SEAFARING WOMEN

Seafaring Women

LINDA GRANT DE PAUW

Houghton Mifflin Company Boston

The author is grateful for permission to quote from "Sea Lullaby" by Elinor Wylie. Copyright 1921 by Alfred A. Knopf, Inc., and renewed 1949 by William Rose Benet. Reprinted from *Collected Poems of Elinor Wylie*, by Elinor Wylie, by permission of Alfred A. Knopf, Inc.

Library of Congress Cataloging in Publication Data

De Pauw, Linda Grant.
  Seafaring women.
    Bibliography: p.
    Includes index.
    Summary: Discusses women at sea throughout history in both feminine and masculine roles, including those of pirate, warrior, whaler, trader, and the greatly expanding roles of recent times.
    1. Women and the sea—Juvenile literature. [1. Women and the sea] I. Title.
G540.D462   1982   910'.88042   82-9254
ISBN 0-395-32434-3   AACR2

Printed in the United States of America
P 10 9 8 7 6 5 4 3 2

TO
JOLIE DIANE DE PAUW
AND
BENJAMIN GRANT DE PAUW

By sailors young and old haply will I, a reminiscence of
*   the land be read,*
In full rapport at last.

. . .

Then falter not O book, fulfil your destiny,
You not a reminiscence of the land alone,
You too as a lone bark cleaving the ether, purpos'd I know
*   not whither, yet ever full of faith,*
Consort to every ship that sails, sail you!
Bear forth to them folded my love, (dear mariners, for you
*   I fold it here in every leaf);*
Speed on my book! spread your white sails my little bark
*   athwart the imperious waves,*
Chant on, sail on, bear o'er the boundless blue from me to
*   every sea,*
This song for mariners and all their ships.

Walt Whitman

Contents

SEAFARING WOMEN

1

The Mists of the Past

SEAFARING WOMEN? Do you mean mermaids? The only
heroines at sea are the ships! Besides, everyone
knows that old-time sailors never allowed women aboard;
they thought females brought bad luck. Certainly the
student of women's maritime history appears, at first, to
be groping for data in a realm dominated by fantasy,
myth, and superstition, where there is no place at all for
real flesh-and-blood females. The flesh-and-blood females did exist: they are the subject of this book. But
before turning to fact, it is worth pausing to consider
the fantasies.

Maritime history, it has been said, is a mixture of
customs records, ships' logs, and sailors' yarns. Before
written documents, there were poetry, oral tradition, and
legend. These are the original forms of all history, and
the earliest methods for seafarers to record their experience. Much of what they handed down was supernatural information. No people have been as superstitious

as those who went to sea, to live or die by the unpre-
dictable whims of wind and waves, totally isolated both
mentally and physically from the dry land that is the
natural habitat of the human species. Although men
vastly outnumbered women at sea, especially on long
deepwater voyages, the world of the seafarer was per-
meated by mystical elements composed of female imagery and natural forces personified as female.

To begin with, the sea itself was perceived as a
woman, and often as not a very nice one. The poet
Swinburne, who wrote, "I will go back to the great sweet
mother, / Mother and lover of men, the sea," was one
of the few writers to detect a warm maternal instinct in
the ocean. The sea is usually seen as coldly indifferent
or even cruel. The sea is always ready to kill, sometimes
for ethical reasons, but at other times out of sheer mal-
evolence. And when the sea killed because her moral
sense was outraged — as when a thief or murderer attempted to travel across her broad bosom — she would
destroy an entire ship to avenge the insult. For that reason, sailors avoided traveling with anyone who seemed
to lack moral integrity — someone, for instance, who
tried to leave port with unpaid bills. Such shipmates
brought bad luck because they offended the sea.

Avoiding traveling with a "Jonah" did not assure
safety. The sea often grew angry for no obvious reason,
and sailors would attempt to buy back her favor by
throwing gifts overboard — even making human sacrifices. In the final analysis, however, the sea did as she
pleased and could be cruel, people felt, as only a woman

could be cruel. The poet Elinor Wylie vividly captured this view of the ocean in her poem "Sea Lullaby":

> *The sea creeps to pillage,*
> *She leaps on her prey;*
> *A child of the village*
> *Was murdered today.*
>
> *She came up to meet him*
> *In a smooth golden cloak,*
> *She choked him and beat him*
> *To death, for a joke.*
>
> *Her bright locks were tangled,*
> *She shouted for joy,*
> *With one hand she strangled*
> *A strong little boy.*
>
> *Now in silence she lingers*
> *Beside him all night*
> *To wash her long fingers*
> *In silvery light.*

Although the tendency to personify the sea as feminine was not universal, it was nearly so. The hero of Ernest Hemingway's *Old Man and the Sea* explained why he felt about the ocean as he did: "He always thought of the sea as 'La Mar' which is what people call her in Spanish when they love her. Sometimes those who love say bad things about her but they are always said as though she were a woman. Some of the younger fishermen, those who used buoys as floats for their lines and had motorboats, bought when the shark livers had brought much money, spoke of her as 'el mar' which is masculine. They spoke of her as a contestant or a place or even an enemy. But the old man always thought of her as feminine and as something which gave or withheld great favors, and if she did wild or wicked things it was because she could not help them. The moon affects her as it does a woman, he thought."

Not only is the sea female, but so is the ship. People felt that ships had distinct personalities. Some ships were said to hate their crews — the H.M.S. *Achilles,* for example, where twelve sailors died in falls from the rigging during a forty-two-month period. Another hostile ship was the *Grace Harwar,* whose bad temper was blamed on her first master's action in preserving his wife's body in the ballast when she died at sea. After that, it was said, the *Grace Harwar* "killed a man on every voyage." Nevertheless, it was thought that a ship's personality could be controlled, to some extent, by taking proper ritual precautions while she was being built and launched. Sailors could also refuse to work aboard a "man-eater," an option they exercised when they were convinced that a vessel was unlucky. Other ships seemed to love their crews and were loved in return. The *Cutty Sark,* most famous of all the nineteenth-century clipper ships, was such a vessel: it has been said that every sailor who sailed on her spoke of that ship with affection. Even at the end of her life, old and neglected, sailing under the Portuguese flag — her name changed to *Ferreira* — she was remembered from earlier days by a visitor who found her personality unchanged. The crew, as fond of her as ever, referred to her by the nickname *El Piquina Camisola* — a translation of the Scots dialect phrase *cutty sark,* meaning "short petticoat."

The strongest emotional tie existed between a ship and her captain. "I felt as proud of my ship as I did of my wife," wrote one nineteenth-century captain who usually took his wife to sea with him. "All sailors do, and Jack's wife feels happy in believing the ship to be her only rival." The notion of a captain being married to his ship was more than a metaphor, and, as one might suspect, the emotional bonding was even stronger for men who went to sea without a human wife. It was the custom in Greece for the skipper to formalize his assumption of command over a new vessel by hanging up a crown of laurel leaves, the symbol of a wedding between a human pair on shore. Indeed, there were few compliments relating to behavior or appearance that a sailor would not apply interchangeably to a ship and a woman. "You have only to *will* her to do something and she responds!" wrote the captain of the *Olympic.* According to the captain of the *Mauretania,* his command had "the manners and deportment of a great lady and behaved herself as such." The perfect ship greatly resembled the perfect wife; the only things she could not do were cook and produce an heir.

As they compared ships to women, sailors compared women to ships. A female with an admirable shape was said to "have a good build on her" or to be "a likely looking craft." A streetwalker who was obviously an old working model and had seen better days was called "a hooker," after *hoeker*, an awkward Dutch fishing boat. And the same type of woman, dressed to the teeth and actively seeking customers, was called a "flash packet" or "fireship," particularly if she was suspected of carrying venereal disease.

In addition to perceiving the sea and the ship as material entities endowed with feminine personalities, seafarers believed in sea goddesses who were distinct from the sea. They were not the sea, but they had powers over the sea. In virtually every part of the world, ancient mythologies and religions gave primacy to water. Although not all deities associated with water were female, most were. From the ancient Greeks to the Aztecs, all of creation, including the gods themselves, was thought to have been born from the waters. The goddess of water was, therefore, mother of all creation. The Aztecs worshiped Chalchithuityene, the Peruvians Mama Cocha, and the Iroquois Ataensic. Pagan Europeans believed that Aphrodite, the goddess of love, arose from the sea, and she was worshiped by the Greeks in seaside chapels. When Christianity took hold Aphrodite continued to be worshiped in the form of the Virgin Mary, known in seafaring regions as "Our Lady Star of the Sea." The pagan sea goddess had many names, one of which, Maria, simplified her association with the Virgin. Other names included Miriam, Mariamne (which means "Sea Lamb"), Marina, and Marian. Marian was also known as the merry maid — as in the tales of Robin Hood — and an alternative form of merry maid was mermaid. All of these sea-love goddesses, not surprisingly, were peculiarly fond of mirrors because water it-self was undoubtedly the original mirror. Even the Judeo-Christian version of creation echoes the imagery of water and reflection: "The earth was without form, and void; and darkness was upon the face of the deep. And the Spirit of God moved upon the face of the waters."

In addition to the major sea goddesses as creators of the universe from a primal ocean, seafaring peoples believed in thousands of minor deities — both male and female — who had greater or lesser powers over wind and waves. Neptune, for example, still presides over special rituals for first-time crossers of the equator in what has become a mere amusement for those who have faith that radio and radar are sufficient to protect them from the dangers of the ocean. He is always ac-companied by his wife, Amphitrite, who is played by a disguised male on ships that carry no females. Less well known today is the god Oceanus, whose sister and wife was Tethys; their three thousand goddess daughters are known as the Oceanides. Nereus, another sea god, fa-thered fifty daughters, the Nereids, who were identified with mermaids.

Seafarers also held other goddesses, not so immedi-ately related to the sea, in high respect. To this day, it is considered bad luck to launch a ship or lay a keel on Friday, the day named for the old Norse goddess Frigg. The superstition connected to Friday long antedates the Crucifixion, which merely confirmed the day's unlucky aspects. Such minor deities, however, could bring good luck as well as bad. In China, the goddess Ma Chua was

a special friend of sailors. Ashes from her shrine lamps
were carried in junks, and during storms, sailors would
call for aid to "Grandmother Ma Chua." In the Pacific,
Ho Hsien-ku, the only female among the eight Taoist
Immortals, has a special relation to seafarers for she, it
is said, invented boats. Finally, the grim Hindu goddess
of death, Deva Lokka, her name corrupted to Davy
Jones's Locker, waits at the bottom of the sea to receive
sailors who have drowned.

As the sea had minor deities who could influence her
actions, so did the ship. Naturally, sailors did their utmost to attract beneficent powers of either sex. Captain
Joshua Slocum, who sailed alone around the world in
1895–1898, had the company of his feminine ship —
"dear old *Spray*," as he called her — who had her own
notions of where the voyage should end, insisting she be
tied up at "the cedar spile driven in the bank to hold
her when she was launched. I could bring her no further
home." But he also had the company of a supernatural
male pilot, who appeared on the deck one night when
Slocum was too ill to steer, identified himself as pilot of
Columbus's ship *Pinta*, and took the helm. When Slocum recovered he found the ship had made ninety miles
overnight in rough seas. Properly appreciative, Slocum
"reached for a bottle of port-wine . . . and took a long
pull from it to the health of my invisible helmsman."

Such ghostly protectors, however, are frequently female. Indeed the Finns believed that a female spirit who
watched and guarded it was aboard every ship. Sometimes the spirit herself attended to a detail neglected by

the crew, but in time of emergency she might show herself and gesture toward a part that needed fixing or a weakness in the ship or gear that required immediate attention.

Belief in a ship's guardian deity went back at least to ancient Rome. The afterdeck of Roman ships, the poop, carried altars set up to honor the vessel's *tutela* or patron goddess. It has been suggested that continuing gestures of respect, such as saluting the flag and the officer of the deck, on modern warships are distantly derived from the Roman practice of genuflecting toward the altars on the stern deck.

In addition to setting up altars, the Romans attempted to attract the patronage of powerful goddesses with symbolic magic. When a Roman trading vessel that sank almost two thousand years ago in the Thames was recovered in 1962, a coin was found fastened in the mast step. The coin, bearing the image of Fortuna, Roman goddess of good luck, with her hand on a ship's rudder, was supposed to assure the patronage of Lady Luck for the merchant ship.

Coins continued to be used as magic charms right into this century, but an even more common way to hold the interest of a friendly spirit to a particular ship was to place an appropriate symbol on the bow. "My guardian deity is yellow-haired Minerva — and may she be such, I pray," wrote the Roman poet Ovid, "and my ship takes its name from a painted helmet on the bow." Minerva, the Roman goddess of war, always wore a helmet over her golden hair and presumably recognized a ship bearing her device as one deserving her particular attention. In the minds of seafaring folk, it was not only supernatural females who had powers to protect and assure the safety of sailors at sea. Magical forces existed in real-life women as well. Although some women used their magical power for evil — water witches, for example, who deliberately caused shipwrecks by casting spells and could best be recognized by their red hair — most real women in seafaring communities used all their supernatural power to support their men. A relic of the old beliefs is the continuing custom of a woman christening a ship about to be launched and in other ceremonies in which a woman's touch is felt to be essential. The Royal Navy, for instance, celebrates the commissioning of a ship with a special cake that is cut with a naval sword by the captain's wife with the assistance of the youngest sailor aboard. The same team cooperates in preparing the traditional Christmas pudding aboard ships of the Royal Navy, each giving it a good stirring for luck before it is cooked.

In the days when people took magic seriously, female powers were put to practical use. The Scots, though they were much troubled by evil witches, approved of and used the power of witches to communicate with ships at sea. If a ship were overdue or the people on shore had an urgent reason to communicate with it, a young girl was encouraged to fall into a trance and send her spirit to the ship at sea. But there was some danger in this operation: if the wind changed while the girl's spirit was off on its mission, she became insane. An always-safe magical ritual was practiced aboard the ships themselves. Homeward bound sailors, at the end of a voyage, dangled a length of rope over the side, to be used by wives and sweethearts whose longing for their men would pull the ship home at supernatural speed. Of course the men's longing for their women helped too, and having "the girls ahold of the rope" put everyone in a good mood. Richard Henry Dana wrote of his time at sea in the nineteenth century, "At each change of the watch, those coming on deck asked those going below 'How does she go along?' and got, for answer, the rate and the customary addition 'Aye! and the Boston girls have had hold of the tow-rope all the watch!' " As the ship raced for home, sailors sang a popular song whose refrain was

> *And it's haul away, girls, steady and true,*
> *Dolly and Molly, Polly and Sue,*
> *Mothers and sisters and sweethearts and all,*
> *Haul away, all the way, haul away, haul!*

There is a popular misconception that seafaring men were commonly misogynistic — that they hated women and that most men went to sea to get away from women. In fact, seamen seem to have been as fond of women as men on shore, and they looked on separation from the opposite sex as one of the hardships of their work. Officers of merchant ships and warships who could take their wives to sea with them if they chose generally jumped at the opportunity, and the efforts of sailors to find something to take the place of normal family life show that few of them thought sex segregation was a happy arrangement. In Fiddler's Green, the mythical heaven of sailors, good-looking women were a prominent feature. While seamen often had to be content with short-term sex with a hired prostitute, sailors idealized the "good" women in their lives — the sweethearts, wives, and mothers who, judging from the drawings, carvings, and poetry produced at sea, were rarely far from their thoughts. Some writers have suggested that the extraordinary strains placed on family life by long separations actually made families in seafaring communities stronger because their members appreciated each other more and held their affections together with prayers and letters, while families not so tested took their relationships for granted.

The love of real women, then, was a magic force for good at sea, and sailors tried to bind it to them in symbolic or ceremonial forms. To touch the pudenda of a sweetheart or wife before sailing was a good-luck charm. So was wearing a tattoo of the name of lover or mother. Some American sailors of the nineteenth century wore a tattoo of a nude woman as a good-luck charm — although if placed properly over a muscle and made to move in an interesting way it also provided a certain amount of entertainment for bored shipmates. United States Navy officers, however, disapproved of such adornment and required sailors to put dresses of red or blue over their naked ladies. This produced the so-called

Miss Liberty tattoo that long identified sailors of the United States Navy.

Another way to bring the feminine presence aboard a ship was in her figurehead. From ancient times, it was common to place a decoration of some sort at the bow of the ship so that other ships or supernatural beings could identify it from a distance. The belief that a ship is itself in some sense a living being, in need of a head and especially eyes, is also ancient and widespread. It became fashionable late in the eighteenth century to have a figurehead directly related to the name of the ship, and throughout the next century figureheads were in their heyday as works of art. Although they could represent men or animals, most were carvings of females, usually bare-breasted.

Well-endowed South Sea island maidens, mermaids, and Indian princesses sailed the seas in effigy, as did carved representations of wives and daughters of New England captains and shipowners. The latter did not flaunt their bosoms quite as openly, but often wore low-cut dresses when they modeled for the artist.

The nudity of figureheads was functional. For some reason, sailors believed, the sea approved of naked women; and, in the absence of real ones, the bare breasts of a carved figurehead were thought to have the power to quiet storms. Perhaps the sea, like the sailors, saw so few real women as to be easily satisfied with a facsimile. Certainly some sailors believed in the domestic spirit that inhabited the figurehead as fervently as any worshiper who saw the lips move in an image of a saint. The captain of the *Princess* observed many of his crew going forward after dark to whisper their troubles into the ears of the lovely figurehead.

Nevertheless, a carving, however lovely, was only a carving. To have a real woman aboard was far better for both practical and magical reasons. Philip Freneau defended the seagoing life from the perspective of a captain of a well-fitted-out ship:

> *Do they ask me what pleasure I find on the sea? —*
> *Why, absence from land is a pleasure to me:*
> *A hamper of porter, and plenty of grog,*
> *A friend, when too sleepy, to give me a jog,*
> *A coop that will always some poultry afford,*
> *Some bottles of gin, and no parson on board,*
> *A crew that is brisk when it happens to blow,*
> *One compass on deck and another below,*
> *A girl, with more sense than the girl at the head,*
> *To read me a novel, or make up my bed —*
> *The man that has these, has a treasure in store*
> *That millions possess not who live upon shore.*

In addition to their real presence as novel readers and turners-down of beds, women, with their aura of continuing life, were symbols of good fortune. Their power to calm storms by exposing themselves naked has already been mentioned. Even stronger magic was embodied by pregnant women; a ship favored by a woman giving birth on the first night out of port, it was said, would never sink.

If women and feminine forces generally were seen as

so valuable and important by sailors, why were women at sea considered bad luck? The answer is that women at sea were not considered bad luck; the notion that sailors ever had such a superstitious belief is a myth of shore folk. As individuals, women could be dangerous or obnoxious shipmates, just as individual men could be. But no one ever seems to have feared that a woman, simply because of her sex, would attract supernatural forces that could harm the ship or her crew. Some groups of people were feared in exactly that way — notably parsons, as Freneau's verse indicates — but among females, only nuns aroused a similar fear.

An instructive example was recorded by the second mate of the *Omba*, which sailed from Shanghai with a clergyman, his wife, and their child. "In the first part of the trip," he wrote, "all had gone well, no one concerned themselves about the proverbial ill-luck which attends the carriage of parsons by sea." But when the *Omba* was stuck in a three-week calm, the captain became convinced the parson was the cause. No one, it seems, gave a thought to the clergyman's wife, but as the calm continued, the mate recalled, "The old man's text as he tramped the poop was loudly spoken and often: 'Oh, if the Lord will only forgive me this once for carrying a parson, I'll never do it any more!' " There are a great many taboos and bad-luck omens at sea. In addition to parsons and such morally tainted people as murderers and debtors, Finns (who were all believed to have supernatural powers) and certain animals and birds were objects of superstitious caution. But women? Never.

Then how did the idea that women at sea are bad luck become current on shore? Some shore folk may have been confused by taboos associated with keel laying and shipbuilding. Because the growing hull was believed to be susceptible to invasion by evil spirits, objects likely to attract the interest of supernatural forces — cross-eyed people, people with red hair or flat feet, parsons, pigs, and rabbits — had to be kept away until construction was complete. Then it was perfectly proper, even desirable, to have a parson bless the vessel and for pigs to be loaded aboard as food during a voyage. Because women embodied magical life forces they, especially virgins and menstruating women, had to be kept away while the ship was vulnerable and under construction. The belief that a menstruating woman would harm anything she touched was not confined to maritime communities where, to this day, it is considered bad luck for a menstruating woman to sew on a sailor's badges. It has been a widespread, persistent superstition, and, according to a survey conducted in 1981, 8 percent of Americans still believe a menstruating woman should stay away from other people. Thus women, even menstruating women, brought no worse luck at sea than they did on shore, and at sea their magical beneficent powers more than compensated for whatever danger they presented for part of each month.

The few cases in which women appear to have been supernatural agents of bad luck turn out, on closer inspection, to illustrate something else. Consider, for example, the case of the *Grace Harwar*, which hated her crews after the captain buried his wife in the ballast. Other ships have turned nasty because bodies of men or boys contaminated them. The conclusion seems to be that what upset the *Grace Harwar* was the presence of a corpse, not the fact that the corpse was female.

The same might be said about the mummy of an Egyptian princess blamed by some for the sinking of the *Titanic*. One might argue that even if the mummy, which some claimed was on the bridge with the *Titanic*'s captain at the fatal moment, had been responsible for the disaster, the supernatural powers were attracted not by its gender but by the curse that protected its original resting place. Unfortunately, although it is certainly the most vivid story of supernatural intervention at sea produced in the twentieth century, the entire tale of the mummy and the *Titanic* is mythical. The mummy of "Unknown Princess from Thebes XXI Dynasty, BM Exhibit 22542" did not sail on the *Titanic* but remained in the British Museum. If the *Titanic* was indeed jinxed by a woman, it must have been by one of the passengers or crew.

That no passengers of either sex appear to have been deterred from sea travel by fear that the presence of a woman on a ship would jinx it suggests that shore folk believed in the superstition no more than sailors did. They merely believed that sailors believed in it, and that belief may have kept a few women from going to sea out of consideration for the poor, ignorant seamen. Two groups of people would have benefited from a superstition that kept women from going to sea: captains who had extramarital interests and shipowners who feared that a captain might not take dangerous risks if the lives of his wife and family were at stake. Perhaps captains with second families in Tahiti or Fiji did, in fact, manage occasionally to convince their wives not to go to sea by explaining that a woman's presence would terrify the crew. Shipowners had the power to order captains to sail alone; but a captain who knew the truth and really wanted her along was unlikely to allow his wife to be deterred by a lie from sailing with him. As for risk taking, plenty of ships were lost with both captain and wife; a captain determined to set speed records did not have to be pushed to greater recklessness.

The most persistent myth respecting seafaring women is that they never went to sea. Indeed, the "women are bad luck" myth appears to be cited most often to explain their presumed absence. Yet anyone with the most cursory knowledge of maritime literature knows that women have gone to sea since Noah took his wife and daughters-in-law with him in the ark. Women, like men, have gone to sea for many reasons. Few, if any, went to prove something about their sex. Most went in clearly defined feminine roles: wife, laundress, cook, nurse, or prostitute. A much smaller number of women assumed male roles and served as sailors before the mast or in positions of command. Seafaring women were a minority among both women and seafarers. But they were real people, not creatures of fantasy. Their history is a significant and badly neglected part of our maritime heritage.

2

Pirates

Pirates are people who steal and murder on the high seas for private reasons and personal benefit. At one time it was considered legitimate for civilians to steal from and murder citizens of enemy nations at sea in wartime, so long as they got formal permission from their own governments. When they did so, they were called privateers, not pirates; and if they were successful on their marauding expeditions, they were hailed as patriots and naval heroes. There have been both women pirates and women privateers, but this chapter deals only with the former. The privateers, who were more respectable, will be discussed in another place.

Although many pirates justified their criminal activities to themselves, blaming wrongs they had suffered in their lives for their choice of an outlaw career, it is their victims who really deserve sympathy. Yet pirates have fascinated writers for centuries in a way that shore-based cutthroats have not. Pirates are often heroes and hero-

ines in novels and plays in which they would more
rightly be cast as villains. It is easy for writers of fiction
to romanticize pirates, partly because hard, factual
knowledge about them is scarce. For obvious reasons,
pirates did not keep written records of their business
activities. Once retired from their grisly profession, pirates did not seek publicity; and they were not likely to
brag to their children about their youthful exploits. Unless crime was a family business, young folks were not
apt to be proud of having a mother or a grandmother
who was a pirate. When pirates did speak out, defend-
ing themselves in court or confessing before being
hanged, they may have told more lies than truth. People
who steal and murder often do. Nevertheless, there is
enough evidence — testimony from victims, records of
legal proceedings, as well as occasional confessions — to
recover the history of some women who have engaged
in piracy, a history that extends through the seven seas
and hundreds of years.

★

One of the first woman pirates known to have operated
in the North Atlantic was named Alvilda; her adventures were originally set down by a twelfth-century
historian, Saxo Grammaticus. Alvilda was a Gothic princess who lived in what is now Sweden. As has often
been the case with princesses, her father, King Sypar-
dus, felt he had the right to marry his daughter off to
anyone he chose. He decided on Alf, son of King Siga-
rus of Denmark. This arrangement did not suit Princess

Alvilda, so she left home, recruited a crew, and went to sea to practice piracy. Her first crew consisted entirely of young women, who must have been a tough, muscular bunch. Gothic ships relied more on oars than on sails for propulsion; and they fought without guns, having only hand weapons. Perhaps the girls had learned their seafaring skills on fishing vessels, which women in many societies have handled in the absence of men; and they had probably learned to kill by butchering farm animals, which was a common chore for medieval housewives. At any rate, they were good at their work; after several expeditions into the Atlantic, Alvilda's pirates began to make a name for themselves.

Alvilda's career got an unexpected boost when her ship encountered another pirate vessel that had recently lost its captain. Alvilda was asked to take command. She agreed, and the combined gang, with approximately equal numbers of men and women, became such a menace to shipping that the forces of law and order became aroused. In particular, Prince Alf of Denmark, who had no idea that the pirate ship terrorizing vessels off the Danish coast was commanded by his supposed fiancée, took out a ship to attack the pirates. A sea battle ensued in which the prince's ship was held off for some time, but eventually the prince's party boarded the pirate ship and killed most of the crew. The pirate captain, dressed for combat in armor and helmet, was brought to the prince. When the helmet was removed, the prince took a long look at his adversary and proposed marriage. Whether she was won over by Prince Alf's asking her instead of her father or was persuaded by the circumstances, Princess Alvilda accepted his proposal and retired from the sea.

*

Leaving out petty criminals, the next female pirate to operate in the Atlantic was Lady Killigrew of Cornwall. Piracy was a tradition in her family and in that of her husband, Sir John Killigrew. She lived in the sixteenth century, at the time of Queen Elizabeth I. For three hundred years the rulers of England had found pirates so useful in wartime that they tolerated a good deal of plain thievery in peacetime to maintain good relations with these aggressive seafarers, who could become privateers at a moment's notice. Indeed, Sir John, who controlled whole syndicates of pirates all around the coast of Great Britain, had a host of royal titles, including Vice-Admiral of Cornwall, Royal Governor of Pendennis Castle, and President of the Commissioners for Piracy. As long as the Killigrews avoided stealing from friends of Queen Elizabeth, they would have no trouble with the authorities.

Sir John and his lady plied their trade diligently for many years, making piratical cruises along the English coast and avoiding confrontations with the law. Then one night in the spring of 1582, Lady Killigrew took out a boat by herself to take a forbidden prize. It was a tempting victim: a German ship, reported to be richly laden with valuable goods, peaceably anchored in Falmouth harbor, easily reached and virtually undefended, feeling secure under the protection of the English crown. But Lady Killigrew wanted the prize. She called up a crew and took the helm of a small boat, guiding it silently to the side of the German ship. Swinging a cutlass, she led the screaming boarders over the side and murdered the entire crew. To the pirates it seemed a good night's work. The cargo was indeed valuable, including two barrels of heavy silver coins. When Queen Elizabeth heard of the attack, however, she was furious. Lady Killigrew and two of her lieutenants were tried, convicted, and sentenced to hang. Having made her point, however, the queen relented. The two men were hanged, but Lady Killigrew's sentence was commuted to a prison term. The queen knew that she might eventually want her services again.

★

A contemporary of Lady Killigrew, and the most famous of all Irish pirates, was Grace O'Malley. She was also known as Granny Wale (sometimes spelled Grana Weil, Graun'ya Uaile, or Granuaile) and is commonly called "Queen of the West" and "the Great Sea Pirate." She was one of the most flamboyant of all pirates, from a nation much given to myth making and poetry, and her history has gathered legend like barnacles. She is said to have buried more than nine tons of treasure, much of which was protected by a curse said to have killed would-be treasure hunters as recently as the present century. A small niche in her tomb on Clare Island holds a skull said to be hers, which is reputed to be

protected against thieves by a still-potent curse. Despite
the overlay of myth and superstition, Grace O'Malley
was unquestionably a real person whose life story hardly
needs fictional elaboration.

Both of Grace O'Malley's parents were seafarers, and
their daughter was born at sea in 1530. The family combined legitimate activities with piracy, and they had for-
tresses in several places to protect their fleets of ships.
Grace grew up on Clare Island off the coast of County
Mayo, where the largest of the O'Malley ships were
moored. While she was still quite young she had an adventure there that marked her for life. The O'Malleys
grazed sheep on the island, and a brood of eagles had
been carrying them off to their aerie high on a cliff.
Grace took it upon herself to end this nuisance by
climbing the cliff and slaughtering the birds. By rights
she should have been the one slaughtered; a bird that
can carry off a sheep is not to be tangled with casually,
especially by a small child. As it was, the talons of the
angry eagles deeply gashed her forehead, and the scars
never disappeared.

It was just after her encounter with the eagles that
Grace first went to sea as a working member of her father's crew. The story is told that her father first refused
her request to sail with him and that she disguised herself as a boy and enlisted without his knowledge. After
she had proved her worth as a sailor, she revealed herself to her father and only then was accepted in her own
right. Actually, it is highly unlikely that any deception
was involved. A girl who can climb a cliff and kill eagles

probably looks boyish all the time; her father must have been used to seeing her in working clothes rather than pretty frocks. Then there were those blazing scars on her forehead; few people alive had anything like that. Finally, Irish ships were crewed by family members; everyone aboard was related to Grace. No strange boy could have infiltrated such a crew. In any case, Grace did go to sea with her father, who trained her to be an expert warrior both on land and on sea. Although she had a younger brother, Grace was her father's heir and took command of the O'Malley fleets and castles after his death.

Ireland was an ideal place to base a pirate empire in the late sixteenth century. There was brisk trade between such ports as Cork and the wealthy nations of Spain and Portugal. The many inlets of the Irish coastline, especially in the south, provided ideal lairs. From such bases, Grace O'Malley pursued her bellicose career, practicing freelance piracy and waging a private war against England. Queen Elizabeth put a price on her head, offering a reward of £500 for her capture. English troops were sent to lay siege to one of her castles, but they could not take it; and the ships of O'Malley's fleet were so powerful that Queen Elizabeth did not dare to attack them.

Between military expeditions, Grace O'Malley found time to marry twice and to bear numerous children. Her second husband persuaded her to become reconciled to the English, and she became an ally of Queen Elizabeth. The queen invited her to visit London, which she did, on the way giving birth to a son at sea. She named the child Tibbot of the Ships, and Queen Elizabeth knighted him as Sir Theobald.

There had been a bit of a fuss at the time of Tibbot's birth. Just after he was delivered, a Turkish vessel attacked O'Malley's ship. The new mother climbed to the deck with a blunderbuss in each hand to repel the boarders. She was obviously not the sort whose maternal instincts made her soft. She was more than a strict parent; she might better be described as ferocious. Once when she and one of her sons were in a boat, being rowed out to Clare Island during a storm, he fell overboard into the rough sea. He managed to grab the side of the boat and began to pull himself back aboard. This did not suit his mother, who took a knife and chopped off his hand. The story is told that when the boy protested, "But I was only going to get back aboard," she snapped back, "If you had been a true O'Malley you'd not have fallen overboard in the first place," and left him, bleeding, to die in the waves.

Grace O'Malley's nineteenth-century biographer, William O'Brien, described his subject as a gracious and charming lady with "healthy transparent cheeks" and "a certain twinkle in . . . merry grey-blue eyes." It seems an odd way to label this rough, scar-faced pirate. Perhaps charm is in the eye of the beholder. Spanish sailors, against whom she won her greatest victory off Shark Island when she was over sixty, saw her differently. She came on deck in her nightgown, her gray hair flying loose down her back, the scars on her face livid, brandishing a sword in one hand and a pistol in the other. Her appearance was so alarming that the Spaniards dropped their weapons, believing they were being attacked by a fiend. Grace O'Malley certainly made an impression on her own age and earned a place in Irish history, but not because of her grace and charm.

*

In the seventeenth and eighteenth centuries, the center of piratical activity was in the Caribbean, where the coves and inlets of the tropical islands made ideal bases. The pirates of the Caribbean had a more comfortable life than most seafaring people. Some discomfort at sea is unavoidable, and pirates suffered from seasickness, damp, heat, cold, storms, shipwrecks, and other nautical nuisances, just like anyone else. They also ran risks other sailors did not. They could be killed while attacking a prize, for instance; but this risk could be minimized by choosing victims carefully, by cultivating a fearsome image to persuade victims to surrender rather than resist, and by becoming expert in the use of pistols and small arms. In any fight with merchant sailors, the odds were overwhelmingly in favor of the pirates; in practice, the chance of a pirate being killed in combat was slight. Indeed, a saying was that pirates were pistol-proof. There was also the unpleasant possibility of being caught by the authorities, which meant being hanged in a particularly elaborate and gruesome manner; but since most pirates had probably committed a few capital offenses on shore before taking up the life under the Jolly Roger, the risk of hanging for piracy did not seem worth brooding about. As far as physical comfort was concerned, pirates had what was, for sailors, a soft life.

Pirate ships were more overcrowded than merchant ships, which would have been a real hardship had the ships remained at sea very long. The overcrowding was unavoidable because, as was the case with warships, pirate vessels needed enough hands aboard both to manage sail and to operate weapons during an engagement. A two-masted pirate sloop, for instance, might carry a crew of two hundred. On a navy ship sailors had no choice about such overcrowding, which meant shortages of food and water, and hot tempers on voyages of months or years. It was generally agreed that sailors in the navy had the worst possible life, but sailors on merchant ships did not fare much better. The food was a constant source of complaint, for while the officers might eat well, the crew was fed cheap and monotonous rations. Pirates, on the other hand, always ate well. The good things they stole from the private stores of merchant captains were available to the entire crew, who were accustomed to indulging themselves in such luxuries as chocolate and brandy. They would head into port whenever a shortage developed that they could not make up by taking a prize. Ships on serious business — the merchant and navy vessels — had to stay at sea, anxious to keep to a schedule and to avoid giving sailors an opportunity to desert. By seafaring standards, then, pirates were a self-indulgent lot. And as sex is generally reckoned one of the

good things of life, it is not surprising that pirate seamen did not deny themselves women.

It is impossible to determine the extent to which
women sailed with pirates. One pirate captain, Bar-
tholomew Roberts, reputedly enforced a rule forbidding
prostitutes — both boys and women — as well as gambling aboard his ship. His puritanical attitude was unusual enough to cause comment. Other captains went
out of their way to make sure their men would have
female companionship. Late in the seventeenth century
a pirate ship from the Caribbean sailed to Africa and
captured a large Danish ship. This vessel was so far superior to their own that the pirates decided to transfer
their operation onto the prize. They traded their original ship for sixty African girls; before putting out to sea,
the new ship was renamed *Bachelor's Delight*. One of
these fun-loving bachelors was eighty-four years old.
Such attitudes toward females were not confined to
Caribbean pirates. In the mid-eighteenth century a
Dutch pirate, Hiram Breakes, who operated in the
Mediterranean, procured "wives" for his crew from a
convent in Minorca. He led the men up to the front
door, introduced himself to the Lady Abbess, and then
each sailor selected a nun and took her away to the
ship. The captain also took one for himself, uncon-
cerned by the fact that he already had a legal wife of his
own back in Holland. Perhaps, though, she was not
worth waiting for. When Captain Breakes returned to
Holland he found himself a widower; in his absence his

wife had been hanged for poisoning their son. Altogether, not a very nice family.

It should not be assumed that all women aboard pirate ships were there against their will. Pirates had homes and families ashore in their Caribbean hideouts, and some wives and girl friends enjoyed going out cruising. Most of these women were probably little more than passengers, standing no watches and expected to keep out of the rigging. Perhaps they took a turn at cooking, and they were probably expected to take up a cutlass or pistol to defend the ship if the worst happened and it was overrun. At least a few women, however, were regular pirate crew members. By far the most famous of these were Anne Bonny and Mary Read who, by coincidence, sailed aboard the same ship in the early eighteenth century. Because they had the bad luck to be captured and brought to trial, we know a great deal more about them than we do about most pirates.

Mary Read's mother had raised her daughter as a boy for a very sensible reason. Her husband was a sailor who went off to sea soon after their wedding and never came back. Some months later she gave birth to a son. Shortly after that, the famous eighteenth-century chronicler of pirates, Daniel Defoe, records, "The Mother, who was young and airy, met with an Accident, which has often happened to Women who are young, and do not take a great deal of Care." Mary was the result of this "Accident." The situation was complicated by the death of Mary's older brother before he was a year old. The sailor husband came from a family that had a bit of money, some of which might be available to support a grandchild. The trouble was that the legitimate grandchild was known to be a boy, and an illegitimate granddaughter could hardly expect to qualify for a family allowance. So Mary's mother dressed the girl in boys' clothing. The disguise easily satisfied her husband's mother, and Mary received an allowance of a crown a week until the old woman died, when Mary was thirteen. After that, Mary would have to work for a living; but she was by then so accustomed to playing a male role that she had formed an unusual ambition. She wanted a military career.

First Mary Read tried the navy, serving as a cabin boy aboard a man-of-war. Then she switched to the army and enlisted as a cadet in an infantry regiment in Flanders. Read was bold and strong and distinguished herself for bravery, but she could not get an officer's commission. For that she would need wealthy friends, and those she did not have. So she left the infantry regiment and joined a regiment of cavalry, hoping to find a greater chance for advancement. Once again she behaved so well in combat that, Defoe tells us, "she got the Esteem of all her Officers." Then something unexpected happened: the ambitious soldier fell in love.

The man who attracted her was the trooper she bunked with. The first sign she gave of having more than comradely feelings for him was becoming unusually concerned for his safety. She insisted on joining him whenever he went out on patrols, even though she was not ordered to go. Other soldiers noticed that she went into danger when she did not have to and thought she was mad. So did the object of her affections. Finally, in the tent they shared, she allowed him to discover that he was bunking with a woman. He was definitely interested. Read, however, had no intention of making her mother's mistake. She wanted an engagement and a formal wedding as soon as the regiment went into winter quarters, and that is what she got.

Understandably, the wedding of two soldiers drew quite a bit of attention. The regiment's officers decided that each of them would give a gift to the bride, "in Consideration of her having been their Fellow-Soldier." This unexpected windfall persuaded the young couple to resign from the service and set up a business of their own. They were able to get their discharges and opened a tavern called Three Horse-Shoes in a building that is said to be still standing near Breda in the Netherlands. All of the officers from their old regiment came in constantly, and for a while the business did very well.

But the good times soon were over. Read's husband died; and when the European wars ended temporarily, business at the tavern slacked off. Read joined an infantry regiment on garrison duty for a while and then, still dressed in male clothing, decided to seek her fortune in America. She embarked on a ship bound for the West Indies, but her bad luck continued, and the ship was captured by English pirates.

It was then the practice of pirates to allow some of their captives to live if they agreed to join the band. Read was the only English person aboard her ship, and she had seafaring skills. Years later, when she was tried for the crime of piracy, she repeatedly swore, according to Defoe, that "the Life of a Pyrate was what she always abhor'd, and went into it only upon Compulsion." Be that as it may, Read signed the articles of the pirate ship, and with only one brief interlude of service on a legitimate privateer, she remained a pirate until her capture in 1720.

Read's new captain was John Rackham, commonly known as Calico Jack because of the brightly colored striped trousers he liked to wear. Rackham already had one woman aboard — his mistress, a lusty teenager named Anne Bonny, who wore male clothing most of the time but made no real attempt to conceal her sex. Read, with her peculiar notions of modesty and chastity, allowed her new shipmates to believe she was a male. She managed to keep her secret until Bonny, who thought she had added a handsome young man to her company of potential admirers, propositioned her.

Here we must fill in something of Anne Bonny's background. Her father was an Irish lawyer named William Cormac who had a roving eye and a taste for riotous living that eventually so exasperated his wife that she left him. He must have been quite a charmer because even though they lived apart, his wife gave him a yearly allowance. Cormac was known to have fathered an illegitimate daughter by the family maid, one Peg Brennan. He thought it would be nice to have his child live with him, but he was afraid that if he took her in openly his wife would finally lose all patience and cut

off his allowance. So he hit on what he thought was a
rather clever plan. He would have the little girl, whose
name was Anne, dress as a boy. Then he could tell people that the child was a relative's son who had come to
be trained as a law clerk.

Unfortunately, Anne was not much good at the masquerade. Unlike Mary Read, who was too young to talk
when she began to pass as a male, Anne could talk very
well, and neither of her parents had taught her to be
discreet. A friend of her father's wife who visited the
house soon found out the truth about the child who lived
there. The consequences were catastrophic. The allowance was stopped, the scandal destroyed Cormac's legal
practice, and the only thing he could think to do was to
take Peg Brennan and his daughter and leave the country. They went to Charleston, South Carolina, to make
a fresh beginning.

Charleston was a good place to make a new start.
Many immigrants had backgrounds they would just as
soon not talk about. Anne's father prospered as a lawyer
and a merchant, and he was able to buy a large plantation. When her mother died, Anne became its mistress
and the heir to her father's fortune. Her father expected
that when she was old enough to think of marriage, she
would attract a splendid husband. Instead, when she still
seemed far too young, Anne decided to marry James
Bonny, a penniless sailor. Her father was furious, certain that the man only wanted his daughter for her
money, and he disinherited her at once.

Bonny took his new bride to the Bahamas. There he

tried to make a living as an informer for the royal governor, turning in suspected pirates for pay. His wife soon grew disillusioned with him, and she quickly found a man who suited her better, the pirate captain Calico Jack Rackham. Rackham was willing to do the decent thing, offering to buy his wife from him if Bonny were willing to sell. Bonny hotly refused. Worse than that, he reported his wife's crime of adultery to the royal governor, who threatened to have her flogged if she did not return to her lawful husband. That was when Anne Bonny joined the crew of Calico Jack Rackham's ship and went off pirating with him. When his mistress became pregnant, Rackham took her to a refuge in Cuba where many pirates had families. After their child was born, she joined him at sea again.

There is no reason to believe that Anne Bonny was a totally promiscuous woman. Defoe reports, "It was certain . . . that once, when a young Fellow would have lain with her, against her Will, she beat him so, that he lay ill of it a considerable Time." Nevertheless, she was more than a little flirtatious, and Captain Rackham kept a jealous eye on her. Doubtless the original members of the crew knew better than to mess with the captain's woman, so when the handsome young prisoner who was Mary Read was taken aboard from the English prize, Bonny had a fresh opportunity to test her attractiveness to men. To her unmistakable overtures Read had no choice, finally, but to respond by confessing "her own Incapacity in that Way." Bonny was disappointed, but then pleased to have a female friend. Rackham, however, flew into a rage over what he thought was going on and told Bonny he intended to "cut her new Lover's Throat." So Bonny told him the truth about Read.

One more of the ship's company was eventually allowed to share Mary Read's secret, for the widow fell in love again. The object of her affections this time was another sailor who had been forced to join Rackham's crew. They enjoyed each other's company and conversation, and finally, "When she found he had a Friendship for her, as a Man," the chronicler tells us, "she suffered the Discovery to be made, by carelessly shewing her Breasts, which were very white." Still concerned with the proprieties that her mother had neglected to her sorrow, Read insisted that she and her lover exchange formal vows, and thereafter she considered him to be her husband. "She looked upon it to be as good a Marriage, in Conscience, as if it had been done by a Minister in Church," she later told a court.

As with her first love, Read was very protective of her sailor husband, who was not so skilled at fighting as she. On one occasion, he quarreled with another member of the pirate crew. The rules of the pirates banned fighting aboard the ship; when two of the crew had a dispute, they were to fight it out with swords and pistols when it was convenient to put in to shore. Read was afraid her husband would be killed, so she picked a fight with the sailor who had challenged him and insisted on a duel two hours before her husband was to fight. Read and the pirate met in single combat, and she killed him on the spot.

The careers of all of Rackham's pirates, including the two women, came to an end in October 1720, when an armed sloop sent out by the governor of Jamaica trapped their ship and boarded it. Soldiers and marines overwhelmed the pirate crew, whose nerve broke, and all but three of them fled below deck. Bonny, Read, and one man continued to resist the boarders even after Captain Rackham had retreated. Infuriated by the cowardice of the others, Read shouted down the hatch for them to come back up and fight like men. When there was no response, she fired her pistols into the hold, killing one man and wounding others. She was unable to rally the pirates to defend themselves, however, and all aboard were taken prisoner.

At their trial some of the pirates could prove that they had joined the crew under compulsion and so were acquitted. Read's husband was among them. Both Read and Bonny, however, were convicted and sentenced to death with all the others. Members of the crew testified against the women, swearing that "in Times of Action, no Person amongst them was more resolute, or ready to board or undertake any Thing that was hazardous." That had obviously been the case during the engagement in which the pirate ship was captured.

In addition, there was testimony from Dorothy Thomas, a woman who had been on a merchant ship boarded by Rackham's crew. She described the two pirates who tried to kill her, saying, "By the largeness of their Breasts, I believed them to be women."

Another witness gave a particularly damning piece of

evidence against Read, except for which the court might have believed her claim that she had been forced to serve on the pirate ship and that her zeal for combat was simply a reflexive habit formed during years of legitimate military service. This witness, a captive on the pirate ship, described his conversation with Read. "What Pleasure," he had asked her, "could she have in being concerned in such Enterprizes, where her Life was continually in Danger, by Fire or Sword; and not only so, but she must be sure of dying an ignominious Death, if she should be taken alive?" Read had replied with a vigorous defense of capital punishment as a matter of good business for the pirates themselves. If it were not for hanging, she said, "every cowardly Fellow would turn Pyrate, and so infest the Seas, that Men of Courage must starve." If it were up to the pirates, she added, "they would not have the Punishment less than Death, the Fear of which kept some dastardly Rogues honest; that many of those who are now cheating Widows and Orphans, and oppressing their poor Neighbors, who have no Money to obtain Justice, would then rob at Sea, and the Ocean would be crowded with Rogues, like the Land, and no Merchant would venture out; so that the Trade, in a little Time, would not be worth following."

Of course, it was only pirates who allowed themselves to be taken alive who had to fear hanging. Anne Bonny's last words to Calico Jack as he was led to the gallows show that she shared Read's feelings on the subject. "She was sorry to see him there," she was heard to say of her lover and the father of her child, "but if he had fought like a Man, he need not have been hang'd like a Dog."

Bonny and Read had fought like men, but that was not the reason they escaped death on the gallows. Though sentenced to die, both were reprieved because they were several months pregnant. Their executions would be delayed until the babies were born. Read, however, contracted a fever in prison and died. As for Bonny, the birth of her child was followed by another reprieve, and then another. Eventually no further trace of her can be found in any official record; she was not hanged, and she did not die in prison. There was time enough for a life full of adventures under a new name, for at the time of her trial she was not yet twenty years old.

*

Bonny and Read were figures of what is often called "the golden age of piracy" in the Caribbean, which ended soon after their capture as it became increasingly difficult for pirates to evade the forces of law and order. Piracy continued in the waters off North America on a much smaller scale than it had assumed in the Caribbean during the second decade of the eighteenth century when, it is estimated, approximately eighty ships and five thousand sailors were engaged in sea robbery. The confession of an American woman named Rachel Wall, who died on the gallows in 1789, gives a picture of the small-scale piracy that must have been very tempting to certain people with low morals and strong stomachs.

Rachel Wall was born in Carlisle, Pennsylvania, and married a sailor, George Wall, who took her to Boston, where she found a job as a servant while he went to sea on a fishing schooner. But following his first voyage after the wedding, Rachel reported, he came back to Boston and "enticed me to leave my service and take to bad company." In addition to her husband, the bad company included five sailors and their female companions. They spent a week drinking until all the money was gone and the fishing schooner on which the men had worked had put out to sea again. Then George Wall suggested piracy. All the men had served aboard privateers during the American Revolution, capturing British ships and dividing the spoils as part of the war effort. That had been patriotic activity. Doing such things in peacetime, as they very well knew, was a capital crime — but that mattered only if one was caught. George invited Rachel to come along, and she accepted.

George Wall had a pirate crew but no ship. He did, however, have an acquaintance who was an invalid and could no longer go to sea. This man owned a fast fishing schooner, which he was willing to lend in return for a share of the catch. Claiming that his party wanted to fish, Wall was able to borrow the vessel. To pass the time until circumstances favored the plans he had in mind, Wall did take his crew fishing. But the first time a storm came up, he put his criminal scheme into operation.

The schooner put in at a tiny harbor at the Isles of Shoals, where she was firmly moored to ride out the rough weather. But as soon as the worst of the storm was past and the winds began to subside, the crew hoisted sail and put out to sea. Once well off the coast and in the path of ships engaged in the New England trade, they disarranged the sails and spars, hoisted a distress signal, and Rachel, conspicuous in her women's clothing, stood on the deck, trying to look like a pathetic survivor on a storm-battered hulk. They did not have long to wait in the busy shipping lane, and soon a schooner from Plymouth drew alongside. The four men aboard were glad to offer Captain Wall, his wife, and the five-man crew passage into port. In return for this kindness, the good samaritans had their throats cut.

The pirates' profit from this escapade was $360 in cash, a good deal of valuable fishing gear and other supplies, plus several hundred pounds of fish ready for market. The booty was transferred to the Wall schooner; the corpses were weighted and thrown overboard; and after a couple of hours of hard work, the Plymouth schooner was damaged enough to sink. When she failed to arrive home, it would be assumed that she had gone down in the storm. Meanwhile, the pirates returned to the Isles of Shoals and a few days later went into Plymouth to sell the gear they had stolen. They had a perfectly plausible explanation of how they had come into possession of it: it had washed ashore at the Isles of Shoals after the big storm a few days earlier. Some ship, they assumed, must have been wrecked nearby.

Five weeks later another hurricane developed, and the Walls went out pirating again. This time the victim was a trading vessel from Penobscot with a crew of seven. The larger numbers aboard called for a slight change in tactics. Rather than accept an offer to carry his charming wife and the others aboard to safety, Captain Wall said, they would prefer to stick with the ship. He would, however, appreciate having the captain and mate come aboard to give him some advice on how to stop a leak in the hold. Glad to oblige seafarers in distress, the pair went aboard where, once in the hold, they were knifed to death. Captain Wall went back on deck and called over to the other ship that their captain wanted some wedges. Two sailors brought over what was requested; when they took the wedges below, they too were killed. This left three unsuspecting sailors alive on the Penobscot ship, and they were easily dealt with. Seven murders produced a profit of $550 in cash from the captain's strongbox and merchandise that was sold in Scituate, Massachusetts, for $70.

The Walls continued their piratical raids into the next year, making a steady income, though by no means a fortune, and murdering dozens of people. The end came as the result of Captain Wall's misjudgment of the vagaries of a storm he was, as usual, attempting to exploit as cover for an attack. Moored at the familiar anchorage at the Isles of Shoals, the schooner waited for a hurricane to subside just enough to make it safe to put out to sea. The sun came out briefly, Captain Wall ordered sail set, and they were off. It turned out, however, that the period of sunshine had been the calm at the eye of the storm. Once at sea, the schooner was hit with the full fury of the wind and rain. This time there was no play-acting. The mainmast snapped and was carried overboard. Captain Wall and one of his men were swept over with it and disappeared in the high waves. When a brig from New York came by the next day and picked up the survivors, the grieving widow they saw on the deck was genuine.

That was the end of piracy for Rachel Wall. The brig dropped her off at Boston, where she was able to get back her old job as a servant. She did not exactly lead a blameless life after that. She formed the habit of slipping down to the waterfront, boarding ships at anchor there, and stealing what valuables she could find. The captain's head — the latrine reserved for the exclusive use of the master of the ship — was often a good place to search. Once she found more than £30 in gold coins wrapped in a black silk handkerchief in the captain's head of a French ship while the captain and his mate were sleeping. On another occasion she discovered the captain's silver watch hanging in that private place.

If one believes this light-fingered lady's dying confession, she was never caught at any of the crimes she committed. But in 1789 she was convicted of robbery and hanged with two other malefactors on Boston Common. Although she confessed herself to be a pirate and a thief, she died protesting her innocence of the robbery. Rachel Wall also insisted that in her pirate days she had never actually murdered anyone. In this respect, she stands in contrast to another woman pirate who was active in both New England and English waters about the same time Wall was hanged and who was decidedly bloodthirsty.

*

Maria Lindsey fell in love at first sight with a sea captain named Eric Cobham, whom she met one day on the main street of her home town of Plymouth, England. After a bit of conversation, he invited her to visit his ship, where he explained his business activities to her. He was a pirate, just back from his first cruise in command. They had taken an East India merchant ship, he told her, that had £40,000 in gold aboard. He explained how he persuaded the captain to turn over the treasure and then ran him through the heart with a sword. His crew killed all the others aboard so there wouldn't be any witnesses. There were terrible screams, he said, lots of blood. It took till midnight to finish them all off. Then they sewed up the bodies in bags full of rocks and dumped them overboard.

Maria was enchanted. She married Captain Cobham the very next day, said good-by to her parents, and went off on her honeymoon on a fourteen-gun cutter headed out into the high seas to send more merchant sailors to the bottom of the ocean in canvas bags.

The marriage of the Cobhams was truly a match made in hell. Maria set herself to mastering the pirate business and developed considerable flair. Once the pirates captured a ship that was carrying a young naval officer. She admired his uniform, so she had him stripped be-

fore she ran him through with her sword. Then she put
his clothing on herself. She was so pleased with the costume that she wore it from then on; when the original
grew shabby, she had new uniforms made in the same
style.

Maria Cobham always took an active part in the fighting when the ship engaged a prize, but murder for her
was not merely a business necessity in the pirate trade;
it was a pleasure and a sport. Once she had the captain
and two mates of a prize tied to the windlass and used
them for target practice, firing eight pistols one after
another from a distance of twenty feet. She never missed.

For twenty years the Cobhams sailed the seas and ac-
cumulated a large fortune. Some of it was buried on
islands off New England and some was in British banks.
Eventually Captain Cobham, who was somewhat older
than his wife, felt it was time to retire, settle down, and
raise a family. His wife agreed, so he went ashore to see
about buying a suitably elegant estate. While he was
gone, Maria Cobham had a final fling. She took the ship
out and overtook an East India merchant vessel off the
coast of Scotland. After a fierce battle, the prize was
taken. The female captain had the survivors put in irons
on the deck and then went into the galley to fix them a
meal. She made poisoned stew. Within an hour all of
them were dead. Maria Cobham disposed of the bodies
and prepared to take her leave of seafaring life.

The Cobhams purchased an estate near Le Havre on
the coast of France. It had its own small harbor, and
the retired pirates kept a small pleasure yacht with some

of their former crew to run it. They became the parents of two sons and a daughter, and after a few years the family had settled into the community so well that when the local magistrate died, Eric Cobham was asked to take his place. The old pirate was now a judge!

Maria Cobham, however, did not adjust as well to retirement. She continued to wear her naval uniform and spent much of her time on the yacht. One day she went for a walk along the cliffs with a bottle of poison in her pocket. Her husband later found it, empty and lying together with her cloak and scarf at the edge of a precipice. Two days later her body was washed ashore.

For some reason, his wife's suicide left Eric Cobham conscience-stricken. Although he had never felt the slightest remorse before, he was now obsessed by the memory of his crimes. He began to spend much of his time in church and eventually wrote out a detailed confession, which he made the local pastor promise to publish after his death. This was done, much to the annoyance of his children and grandchildren, who would have preferred to have the story of their wicked ancestors buried with them. They did their best to keep it off the market by buying up every copy they could lay their hands on.

*

In the nineteenth century the greatest opportunities for pirates lay in the Pacific, and seafarers from many nations enjoyed a life of crime in Asian waters, including one Mary Lovell, who commanded a ship with the romantic name *Moonraker*. But the greatest pirates of the

Pacific were Chinese, and the greatest Chinese pirate was a woman named Hsi Kai Ching Yih. At the height of her career in the early years of the nineteenth century, she commanded almost two thousand ships and more than fifty thousand pirates. Because of the sheer magnitude of her operation, she must be considered the greatest pirate, male or female, in all history.

The tradition of piracy of which Madame Ching was a part began in the year 1799, when spring floods destroyed the crops over a wide area in southern China. The people living by the sea were starving; the population was far too large to survive on the fish their few boats could bring in. Meanwhile, in the distance, they could see Portuguese and English trading ships carrying vegetables, fruit, and meat to more fortunate people who could afford to buy. One day, one of these ships was wrecked. Farmers and fishermen scrambled into their little boats and went out, hoping to salvage some of its cargo, but when they got there they found sailors still guarding it. Frustrated and hungry, so it is said, the crowd fell on the crew and murdered every last one of them, bringing the badly needed food home to their village.

Although begun in a time of dire need, the practice of attacking trading ships off the South China coast soon became a habit. At first the activity was disorganized; every little boat had its own pirate chief. Within a few years, however, one man systematized the operation and made it into a big business.

Ching Yih was captain of a rather run-down twenty-foot junk with a crew of twelve. He, like others, engaged in sporadic attacks against ocean-going traders. Yet he was so successful that other pirates asked to join him, and soon he was in command of a fleet. At first the authorities at Peking considered Ching's raiding to be no more than a mild annoyance, but in 1807 they sent forty warships against his armada. Ching captured twenty-eight of them and sank almost all the rest. A power to be reckoned with, Ching was now ready to take a wife.

The pirate chief's method of courting would not seem to have promised much for his intended bride. Ching's gangs did not confine themselves to sea robbery, but made raids inland as well, where their booty included slaves. When the chief decided he wanted a wife, twenty choice females from recent expeditions were brought before him, securely tied up, so he could look them over and take his pick. Hsi Kai caught his eye immediately.

Hsi Kai was a large woman, the Chinese historians tell us, taller than most women of her race and her feet had not been bound. Her body was voluptuously rounded, she was graceful as a dancer, and as one source says, "Before the beauty of her face the eyes of men grew confused." Wanting to get a better look at this magnificent creature, Ching Yih ordered that she be untied. If he had been expecting a sweet disposition, he was in for a surprise. As soon as she was free, Hsi Kai lunged at the pirate chief, clawing at his face with her nails, and came close to blinding him before she was pulled away.

Some men might have been put off by such a greeting, but Hsi Kai's aggressive temperament made her all the more attractive to Ching Yih. Yet he knew that this woman could not be taken against her will; she would have to be persuaded to marry him. He offered her jewels, cosmetics, rich clothing, and slaves; he described in glittering detail the life of luxury she would enjoy if she would consent to be his wife. That wasn't quite enough, Hsi Kai told him. If she became Madame Ching, she'd want a full half share of all his property and, in addition, joint command of the pirate fleet. Truly a woman after his own heart! Ching Yih agreed.

The Ching fleet was divided into six squadrons — red, blue, yellow, green, black, and white. Madame Ching took command of the red and then the white squadron. Where she learned the art of command at sea is a mystery, but within a few months she was as greatly feared as her husband. Her marriage, however, did not last long. Late in 1807 Ching's squadron was caught in a typhoon, and Madame Ching became a widow.

A Chinese historian described the meeting of the pirate captains held after Ching Yih's death. Madame Ching attended, dressed in the chief's uniform: a robe of purple, blue, and gold, embroidered with gold dragons and bound with a wide sash into which she had thrust several of her deceased husband's swords. She wore his war helmet on her head. The significance of this costume was clear enough: she meant to assume command. "Look at me, captains," she said to the assembled group. "Your departed chief sat in council with me. Your most powerful fleet, the White, under my command, took more prizes than any other. Do you think *I* will bow to any other chief?" No one wanted to argue the point with her. So Madame Ching carried on in her husband's place, and the pirate empire expanded and prospered even more greatly than it had before.

Although Madame Ching was celebrated for her battle exploits, her success owed even more to her administrative ability. She continued the general pattern of organization her husband had developed, with the fleet divided into squadrons, each flying its own colors and under the command of a leader who answered to the chief. The squadron leaders were known by such nicknames as "Scourge of the Eastern Sea," "Jewel of the Whole Crew," or, in one peculiar case, "Frog Meal." All of the ships were bound to obey Madame Ching's regulations, which she had posted aboard even the smallest ship of the fleet. Among these regulations was one decreeing, "No person shall debauch at his pleasure captive women taken in the villages and open places, and brought on board a ship; he must first request the ship's purser for permission, and then go aside in the ship's hold. To use violence against any woman, or to wed her without permission, shall be punished with death."

Provisioning the large number of people attached to the Ching fleet was a major logistical problem. Indiscriminate raiding of shore communities would make the local population so hostile that they could endanger the continued operation of the pirates' business. Or if all the country people were killed or sold as slaves, there would be no food grown in the fields, leaving the pirates with money but nothing to eat. Madame Ching's solution was to enter into agreements with hundreds of farmers who were hired to grow grapes and rice, and she made similar arrangements to be sure she would always have enough gunpowder and naval stores. One of her regulations was that any pirate who attempted to steal from these shore-based employees of the Ching business would be executed.

Madame Ching directed such a large-scale operation that, contrary to the usual practice of pirates, she encouraged written records. The great warehouse where plunder was stored was presided over by a personage known as "Ink and Writing Master." He was in charge of seeing that every item stolen by the pirates was carefully recorded in a register. When a pirate wished to make a withdrawal from the warehouse, written permission from a squadron leader was required.

The pirate chief herself did not spend much time ashore, and she was by no means the only woman to sail with the fleet. Richard Glasspoole, an officer of the British East India Company ship *Marquis of Ely*, who was captured by the pirates in 1809, wrote a description of life aboard one of Madame Ching's ships. "The Ladrones," as he called them, "have no settled residence on shore, but live constantly in their vessels. The after-part is appropriated to the captain and his wives; he generally has five or six. With respect to conjugal rights they are religiously strict; no person is allowed to have a woman on board, unless married to her according to their laws. Every man is allowed a small berth, about four feet square, where he stows his wife and family." According to Glasspoole, these people ate such peculiar things as white rat meat and caterpillar soup and spent all their free time gambling and smoking opium.

When there was fighting to be done, however, both women and men were fierce combatants and resisted repeated efforts by the Chinese emperor to put them out of business. The heroine of one engagement was a pirate wife who stuck to her post at the helm, even after the ship had been boarded, and then fought with two cutlasses, killing and wounding several of the emperor's sailors before being felled by a musket ball and taken prisoner.

Madame Ching was never defeated. Peace came to the coast only when the emperor of China bought her off, offering not only amnesty but command of part of the imperial fleet, a palace, and high honors for her and her captains, including the man she had taken as her second husband. "If there is aught of the woman-heart in you," a Chinese historian quotes the emperor's emissary as saying, "you will one day want peace and offspring. What say you?" Hsi Kai said yes. Eventually she retired from the sea entirely, went to live in the palace provided by the emperor, bore three sons and one daughter, and spent her last years in the less demanding work of a smuggler.

"And from that period," writes the Chinese historian, "ships began to pass and repass in tranquility. All became quiet on the rivers, and tranquil on the four seas. People lived in peace and plenty. Men sold their arms and bought oxen to plow their fields. They burned sacrifices, said prayers on the tops of hills and rejoiced themselves by singing behind screens."

3

Warriors

THERE IS A PERSISTENT MYTH that war has always been an all-male affair and that women in combat zones, whatever their activities, were "civilians" and not "warriors." This becomes a confusing distinction in practice, because men and women under fire often do the same things. It is particularly confusing in the case of naval warfare, because at sea everyone aboard — male or female, gunner, carpenter, or nurse — is quite literally in the same boat. When a ship is fired upon, everyone aboard is at war. This chapter deals with women on warships.

In the past, some of the women aboard warships were civilians; others had an official rating. When ships saw action, some women in both categories were assets and others liabilities. Exactly the same thing may be said of the males aboard.

The history of naval warfare usually focuses on admirals and captains. In recent times women have not been in the high command except in the irregular warfare waged by privateers and revolutionaries. In ancient times, however, when the ruler of a nation decided who should command, queens and other women of exalted status could decide to direct operations at sea themselves. Women commanders figured in two of the most famous sea battles of ancient times — the Battle of Salamis in 480 B.C. and the Battle of Actium in 31 B.C.

In the fifth century B.C., Persia was at war with Greece, with the Persian king Xerxes leading the invasion. Artemisia, the queen of Caria in southwestern Asia Minor, brought five ships to assist in this effort; other rulers brought more, but hers were among the fastest and best equipped in the fleet. Her squadron demonstrated its capabilities during three days of fighting, during which a Greek scouting galley was captured. She was a cautious commander, however, and she advised King Xerxes not to engage the Greek fleet. Artemisia was a queen, but not a feminist, and she spoke as an admiral. "Spare your ships," the Greek historian Herodotus quotes her as saying, "and fight no battle on sea; for the enemy's men are as much better than your men on sea as men are than women." She was the only one of Xerxes' advisors to take this position, however. The Persian force engaged the Greeks at Salamis and were thoroughly defeated. Only Artemisia was able to save her ship and she was the only senior officer to survive. Xerxes, watching from the shore, exclaimed in astonishment that the men had behaved like women and the women had displayed the courage of men.

If Artemisia was an able commander frustrated by a

less perceptive superior, Cleopatra was just the opposite. In 31 B.C., the Roman fleet of Octavian faced the
combined fleets of Anthony and Cleopatra off the coast
of Egypt. The advice of the admirals was not to risk a
sea fight, but as Xerxes had done, Cleopatra overruled
the voices counseling caution. On the day of battle, she
went out with the fleet in her own galley, a splendid
craft, bright with paint and gilding, carrying purple sails,
and flying flags and streamers in the wind. The oppos-
ing fleets appeared to be evenly matched until, for some
reason, Cleopatra's nerve broke, and she ordered her
galley to flee. Assuming that the queen's ship's leaving
signaled a general retreat, all sixty Egyptian ships followed her. The battle was lost by default, and with the
battle the war was lost too.

Artemisia and Cleopatra are the only women mentioned in books on great sea battles. Other women have
exercised command at sea, but on a humbler scale. Although the outcome of a war and the course of history
did not depend on the performance of their ships, they
are, perhaps, a bit more inspiring than these two great
women admirals, because they had their share of victories. They did not command the fleets of great nations,
but those of private navies, which, except for their political orientation, resemble the pirate fleets of Madame
Ching and other outlaws. On sea as on land, women are
far more likely to rise to command in war in units peripheral to the central military organization.

There was a lot of peripheral fighting during the Middle Ages, and anyone who owned a ship and was willing

to risk it could get into a war. Grace O'Malley, the great Irish pirate, occasionally used her fleets for political purposes. Another was Jane de Belleville, a French noblewoman, who supported the English invasion of Brittany in 1345 because her husband had been executed by the French as an English spy. Seeking personal revenge, which incidentally benefited the English, she sold her jewels, bought and outfitted three ships, and then cruised along the coast of Normandy, attacking French vessels and ravaging the countryside. This fine lady was often seen standing amid the ruins of a Norman village with a sword in one hand and a flaming torch in the other, ready to burn to the ground every building still standing.

The activities of privateers were recognized as an important supplement to the operations of regular navies well into the nineteenth century. Privateers were licensed by their governments to attack enemy shipping, and women were occasionally found either in command or in the crew. Fanny Campbell was among the first captains to take private craft into service against the British during the American Revolution. Some months before the war began, this young woman from Lynn, Massachusetts, went to sea disguised as a man, serving as second officer on an English merchant brig, the *Constance*. Her reasons for this had nothing to do with either politics or trade but were entirely personal. She had recently learned that her childhood sweetheart, William Lovell, was in jail in Cuba; he had escaped from a pirate ship, which had captured the ship he served, and was himself charged with piracy. Fanny Campbell signed on aboard the *Constance* with the idea of taking straightforward Yankee-style action to free her man.

Of course, the captain of the *Constance* knew nothing of this, and in any event he would not have been likely to divert his course to assist in a jail break. Fortunately for Campbell's plans, however, neither the captain nor his first mate was at all popular with the crew. Indeed there was some suspicion, which Campbell encouraged, that the captain meant to take his entire crew to England, where they would be impressed into the British Navy. Campbell led a successful mutiny and was confirmed as commander of the stolen brig. That automatically meant that she and the entire crew had become pirates.

Several days later, the *Constance* encountered a British bark, the *George*. The captain of the *George* sensed something wrong about the *Constance*, concluded she was a pirate, and, feeling confident of the *George*'s superior firepower, attacked her. The engagement had an unexpected conclusion, however; the *George* became a prize of the *Constance*, and they sailed on to Cuba together.

The rescue attempt was a success; not only William Lovell but ten other jailed Americans were freed. Fanny Campbell had a happy reunion with her sweetheart, but no one else was told that the officer everyone called "Captain Channing" was not quite the man they thought he was. Back at sea, the *Constance* and the *George* soon took another prize, a British merchant ship that had interesting news: formal war had begun between England

and America. Therefore Campbell's ships had an opportunity to escape the stigma of piracy by becoming legitimate privateers in the American cause. All but four members of the crews of the *Constance* and the *George* readily agreed to become honest men again, even if they would be considered traitors to Great Britain should the war go the wrong way. Fanny Campbell now commanded a pair of private warships, which the next day captured a British sloop-of-war.

The *Constance* and the *George* sailed back to Massachusetts, putting in at Marblehead because British troops had occupied Boston. While the legal papers commissioning them as privateers were being drawn up, Fanny Campbell and William Lovell went home to Lynn and were married. William Lovell continued to privateer throughout the war, but Fanny Campbell began to raise what would eventually be a very large family. None of the children was anxious to publicize their mother's part in naval warfare.

Some years after Fanny Campbell retired from the sea, another woman commanded the French privateer *La Baugourt*, which operated against English shipping in the West Indies. But even on privateers, the odds were against women giving orders; they mostly took them. Why did women embark on privateers? Some probably enlisted of their own free will, as women did on other ships, either disguising themselves as men or finding a captain to whom sex was no barrier. Deborah Sampson, the American woman who is best known for having served in uniform in Washington's army during the

Revolution, considered enlisting on a privateer before settling on the infantry. She had some conversation with the captain of a cruiser in a tavern in New Bedford, Massachusetts. He offered her a place as his "waiter" and even advanced her some money. But she asked around and decided not to sail with him after all, for "she was informed that, although he used much plausibility on the shore, it was changed to austerity at sea."

Some women were coerced into the service. The *Duke*, a British privateer operating in the Pacific in the early years of the eighteenth century, had on board several black women, most likely slaves, who served as cooks. The captain seemed to be perfectly satisfied with their cooking, although one of the women was whipped "to make her modest and well behaved."

Mary Anne Talbot, of whose career more will be said later, enlisted on a French ship, supposing it to be a legitimate trading vessel. It turned out to be privateering against the English, and Talbot was beaten when she refused to fight against her own people. She was rescued from this service when the privateer was taken by a British warship, and Talbot became part of a regular navy crew.

Sarah Bishop of Long Island, New York, was the victim of a British raiding party in 1778. Rape had become an everyday event in the war zones; when Bishop was taken aboard a British privateer, she became a member of the crew with certain additional duties. Although she handled the wheel and stood watches, she was also expected to be a communal sex object. Eventually she and the captain of the privateer came to an understanding, after which she was strictly the captain's woman. The captain was killed, however, in an engagement with an American privateer, and it was another six months before Bishop found an opportunity to escape. Two years after her capture, Sarah Bishop slipped over the side of the ship and swam ashore at Stamford, Connecticut. Her experience had been so traumatic that she could not bear to return to normal human society. She made her way to Ridgefield, Connecticut, and climbed to a rocky cave, where she lived the rest of her life as a hermit.

Bishop had become a seagoing prostitute against her will. The women who volunteered to practice the world's oldest profession at sea found the opportunities greater and the pay better in the regular navy.

In the great days of fighting sail, the regular navy was overwhelmingly a man's world. Although the army and sometimes the marines had women's branches of the service, made up of wives who drew pay and rations and traveled with their men, there was no such provision for the navy. A fair number of navy wives went with their men in spite of the rules, but it was much more difficult for a sailor to have a normal family life than for a man in any other military occupation.

Even today, sea duty puts a strain on families; but while modern sailors rarely stay away more than a few months and have frequent opportunities to send letters and even to make phone calls home, eighteenth-century sailors could be totally cut off from their loved ones for as long as five years at a time. Both officers and ordinary sailors suffered from separation, but it was harder on the sailors. Not only were officers more likely to be allowed to bring their families to sea, they were also the only men aboard certain to have shore leave in port. British sailors of the eighteenth and early nineteenth centuries were impressed, that is, forced, into service. Consequently, officers expected them to desert at the slightest opportunity. To prevent their desertion, sailors were confined aboard ship even in port.

Naval officers, like other members of the ruling class ashore, firmly believed that poor people did not share their capacity for delicate emotions. Modesty, self-respect, and affection were not attributed to the lower orders. It did not occur to those in authority that a seaman might want to go ashore to check on his old mother, or to be sure his sister got the money he wanted her to have from his wages, or have any other selfless thoughts. They even doubted that marriage bonds could be sacred to poor people. They recognized only one need in a sailor who had been a year or more at sea — raw sex. That they would provide, and the circumstances under which they provided it well illustrate the contempt they had for the poor of both sexes.

"I am now happily laid up in matrimonial harbour, blest in a wife and several children," wrote one old sailor who had done his time in the Royal Navy, "and my constant prayer to heaven is, that my daughters may never set foot on board of a man-of-war." One might expect a common sailor to be insensitive to the indignities forced on the poor women of certain seaside towns by the arrangements that were not merely tolerated but actually encouraged by the Royal Navy. But this one was not. "These poor unfortunates are taken to market like cattle," William Robinson, using the pseudonym Jack Nastyface, wrote with feeling in 1836, "and, whilst this system is observed, it cannot with truth be said, that the slave-trade is abolished in England." The lawful wives and daughters of sailors were, in the eyes of officers, virtually indistinguishable from common prostitutes, and when a man-of-war put into port the "needs" of the men were met by bringing females aboard by the boatload.

Women were not physically forced aboard His Majesty's ships, but there was a taint of compulsion about the operation. One had to board the boats to visit a husband or lover and get a badly needed part of his pay. For poor, unattached women, prostitution was usually the best-paying occupation available when jobs were scarce and prices high. Neither wives nor prostitutes had money to pay their way out to the ships in the harbor, so they had to go out together as cargo on what were called bumboats. A wife too proud to mix with prostitutes would have to stay on shore. The owners of these boats sold many items intended to tempt newly paid sailors to part with their cash, like tobacco, candies, and articles of clothing; but their hottest selling item was women. For each one chosen by a sailor, the boatman would collect a "fare" — usually about three shillings.

A woman whose fare was not paid by her sailor husband or some newly attracted sailor lover had to be taken ashore again and was a dead loss to the carrier. Consequently, the boatman inspected the women carefully before permitting them to board. He "surveys them from stem to stern . . . and carefully culls out the best looking, and the most dashingly dressed; and, in making up his complement for a load, it often happens that he refuses to take some of them, observing, (very politely) and usually with some vulgar oath; to one, that she is *too old;* to another, that she is *too ugly;* and that he shall not be able to *sell them;* and he'll be d——d if he has any notion of having his trouble for nothing." Having made it to the side of the ship, a woman wishing to visit still had to pass inspection by the officers. It was common for a lieutenant to look over the boatload of females, just as he would a cargo of foodstuffs, and, to protect the reputation of the ship, permit only good-looking, well-dressed, and carefully painted women to mount the ladder. Finally, before a sailor was permitted to take a woman below — whether his wife, fiancée, daughter, or brand-new "friend" — she had to be examined by the assistant surgeon to be sure she was not infected with venereal disease.

A man-of-war always carried a much larger crew in proportion to her size than other ships did; often five or six hundred men were aboard when the bumboats loaded with women came alongside. In a few minutes, the number of bodies aboard would double. Indeed, women might actually outnumber the men. "It is frequently the case that men take two prostitutes on board at a time," sniffed a disapproving officer. And sometimes a sailor paid his shillings for both a wife and a daughter to visit. In any event, a warship in port usually had hundreds of women aboard — more or fewer according to its size; the *Royal George*, by no means the largest ship of the time, had three hundred females aboard when she sank in Portsmouth Harbor in 1782.

It is surprising that the ships did not sink more often because the women's boarding was the signal for the beginning of a wild party during which virtually all shipboard discipline broke down. First of all, the women supplemented prostitution with bootlegging. At sea, the consumption of alcohol was tightly rationed, and the bumboat owners were not permitted to sell it to sailors in port. But the women took advantage of their voluminous skirts to conceal containers filled with gin, rum, or brandy. The marines were supposed to prevent this smuggling, but it was an impossible task.

A pressed sailor serving aboard the *Salvador del Mundo* recalled how the wife of a newly pressed man was caught carrying rum when she visited the ship before it sailed from Plymouth. As the ship's corporal helped her up the ladder from the bumboat, he "took it into his head that the calves of her legs, at which he had been taking an unmannerly peep, were rather more bulky than chaste statuary required. 'I am afraid, my good woman,' said he, 'that your legs are somewhat dropsical; will you allow me the honour of performing a cure?' " He then took out his knife and slit her stocking. "The point of the knife gently pierced the skin, not of the leg, but of the bladder that was snugly secured there . . . Colour

and smell bore ample testimony that the blood of the
sugar cane had been shed."

The carousing that followed offended the more squeam-
ish officers, but appears to have been thoroughly enjoyed by the participants. Sailors dancing with their
guests were a popular subject with shipboard artists.
Certainly, had they been given a choice, they would have
preferred to have their party ashore, but as they were
not free to choose they did the best they could, accepting the crowding and lack of privacy as unavoidable.

Those who did their courting and their partying in
more pleasant surroundings could afford to disapprove.
"The whole of the shocking, disgraceful transactions of
the lower deck it is impossible to describe," wrote an
officer, "the dirt, filth, and stench; the disgusting conversation; the indecent, beastly conduct, and horrible
scenes; the blasphemy and swearing; the riots, quarrels,
and fightings, which often take place, where hundreds
of men and women are huddled together in one room,
as it were; and where, in bed (each man being allowed
only sixteen inches breadth for his hammock), they are
squeezed between the next hammocks, and must be witness of each other's actions; can only be imagined by
those who have seen all this . . . Let those who have
never seen a ship of war, picture to themselves a very
large and low room (hardly capable of holding the men)
with five hundred women of the vilest description, shut
up in it, and giving way to every excess of debauchery
that the grossest passions of human nature can lead them

to; and they see the deck of a seventy-four gun ship upon the night of her arrival in port."

The party, however, lasted longer than a single night, for the women would remain aboard until the ship was ready to sail. The chaplain of the *Assistance*, who was more understanding of the conditions forced on the crew, described the state of the ship prior to a Mediterranean cruise: "Hither many of our seamen's wives follow their husbands, and several other young women accompany their sweethearts . . . so that our ship was . . . well furnished but ill-manned, few of them being well able to keep watch had there been occasion. You would have wondered to see here a man and a woman creep into a hammock, the woman's legs to the hams hanging over the sides or out of the end of it." Somehow, the captain had to work the presence of these guests into his shipboard routines.

The day began with the boatswain's mates rousing the men with the shout, "Show a leg! Out or down!" A smooth leg or a woman's stocking identified a female, who would be left to sleep. The possessor of a hairy leg, however, had to hit the deck or the lashings of the hammock would be cut, tumbling him down. The officers would then do what they could to get the sailors to perform the tasks that must be done even in port — maintaining the ship, exercising at the guns, and getting ready for the coming voyage. The wives might spend the day mending their husbands' clothing, but most of the women had no useful work to do and passed the time drinking and fighting. On the larger ships, an attempt was made to prevent the women from distracting the crew during working hours by confining the visitors to a compartment under the lower gun deck in which the surgeon treated the wounded during battle. Such crowded quarters led to short tempers, and frequently the female battles were so loud that the marines had to go below to break them up. The sailors came to call the surgeon's station the "cockpit," after the cockpits on land in which fighting cocks fought to the death for the amusement of spectators. When the marines identified major combatants by their scratched faces and torn clothing, the offenders were sent ashore on a bumboat.

Of course, most of this activity was strictly against regulations. *Regulations and Instructions Relating to His Majesty's Service at Sea* specifically stated "that no women be ever permitted to be on board but such as are really the wives of the men they come to; and the ship not to be too much pestered even with them." In 1817 even wives were forbidden to live on board, but the regulations were a dead letter for most of the century. Navy reforms in the years 1860–1870 were supposed to banish women from warships. Although occasional violations continued, officers no longer condoned them openly, as they had in earlier years. When impressment ended and men could be allowed shore leave, there was less need for visiting privileges in port.

Eventually the ship would be ready to sail, and it was time to say good-by. The sailors and their women did their best to keep up their spirits on what was a sadder occasion for some than for others. Perhaps one or two dozen new marriages had been contracted during the days in port, and even those men who were not married and had no such thing in mind regretted leaving the relatively free life at anchor for the austerity of life at sea. As the women went over the side, salutes might be fired and the ship's band play such tunes as "Loath to Depart" or "Maids, Where Are Your Hearts?" Some sailors might hand their ladies a bunch of onions, suggesting they would not cry at parting without their aid. But many tears were sincere enough. Some of the women would walk overland to the next port of call if the ship was scheduled to stop at another home port before heading out to sea, hoping for a last visit before their men went back to war. All women dependent on a husband's pay would wonder if he would live to reach home again or if this was a final parting that might force them to take up the life of the prostitutes with whom they were rowed back to land. A few women, however, had no need to say good-by. Seaman John Wetherell recalled that the captains with whom he sailed in the early years of the nineteenth century issued orders "to send all the girls on shore except one woman to each mess, and the married women certainly to have the preference." Competition for this limited number of slots was fierce, and as the shiploads of weeping women pulled away, one of the lucky few might run aloft into the rigging and wave her petticoat triumphantly.

Captains were not supposed to take any women to sea without permission from the admiralty or from a senior

officer. But many captains, accustomed to enjoying absolute authority at sea, ignored this restriction. There
was a bit of inconvenience, of course, in that the women
could not be listed on the official records as women carried legitimately could be, and there would have to be
fudging with the rations to feed them.

Captains appear to have dealt with this problem calmly
enough; but it is frustrating to historians because the
women's names appear in the documents only when
some unusual event made it impossible to ignore their
presence. Some attention had to be paid, for instance,
when a female body was discovered sewed up in a hammock in the bread room of a man-of-war. And it was
impossible not to take official notice when a midshipman aboard H.M.S. *Alexander* murdered his mother in
the presence of his wife and several other women. He
stabbed her right through her corset stays, they testified
at his court-martial. Any attempt to discover the iden-
tities of the women who went to sea with the acquies-
cence of the captain, their exact numbers, or their duties is frustrated by this erratic documentation. The best
that can be done is to trace an outline, admitting that
the most vivid details in the surviving record may well
be exceptional.

Who were the women who sailed on warships? Some
testimony suggests that they were nothing but whores.
One officer described his experience on two ships to
which he was posted in the first decade of the nineteenth century. Nine women were aboard the first. The
captain and first lieutenant mustered them for inspec-

tion on the forecastle every Sunday, but that appears to have been the only discipline imposed on them. Two or three of the women were so unmanageable that the captain put them off aboard a passing brig, to be carried back to England. Most of the other women, declared this witness, were completely promiscuous: "Of one, I recollect its being stated that she admitted nineteen men to her embraces in one night." This officer's next assignment offered him no better opinion of his female shipmates, who behaved at sea as they did in port, "being almost continually drunk, spirits being given them by the officers, mates, and midshipmen, in payment for their occasional visits."

Prostitutes, however, do not appear to have constituted a significant percentage of women on warships if only because, whatever his personal morals, a captain recognized that the relaxed discipline that worked in port would be dangerous at sea, especially in wartime. Prostitutes were put off when the ship left harbor, and those females remaining — excluding for the moment those who sailed disguised as men — fell into one of three categories: passengers, captain's servants, and women of the army who were wives of marines or soldiers in transport.

Officially approved passengers are recorded in ships' records. Well-connected people of both sexes could gain approval for their passage in a warship. In 1798 Captain Horatio Nelson carried both the queen of Sicily and Lady Hamilton, together with their distinguished husbands, as passengers aboard H.M.S. *Vanguard*. At the same time Captain Thomas Fremantle had the British ambassador, Sir Gilbert Elliot, and a family named Wynne aboard H.M.S. *Inconstant*. In due course, Miss Betsey Wynne became the wife of Captain Fremantle, and Lady Emma Hamilton became the mistress of Captain Nelson — but not during their voyages.

Captains sometimes chose to take their wives or other female relatives to sea, although we are not likely to learn of this from official records unless some unusual event occurred. Anne Chamberlayne, for example, is remembered only because she refused to obey the orders of her brother, captain of the *Griffin*, when he told her to go below during a fleet action. She remained on deck for six hours — some sources say she participated in the fighting — and only when the battle was won did she go below to the more womanly work of assisting the surgeon in the cockpit. Had she gone below in the first place, no record would have mentioned her presence.

Another captain kindly offered his sister, Mary Skinner, passage aboard the *Princess Royal* so she could marry the man who was waiting for her in the United States. She and her maid passed the time sewing up her silk wedding dress — until halfway across the Atlantic, the *Princess Royal* was attacked by the French privateer *L'Aventurier*. The British ship suffered heavy casualties and the cockpit was soon overflowing. Miss Skinner and her maid first made themselves useful by setting up an additional ward for the wounded in the bread room. When the ship ran short of cloth for the bags in which gunpowder was wrapped prior to being rammed down the gun barrels, they cut up the wedding dress, recognizing that, for the moment, war must come before love and leaving a story worth repeating.

A captain might permit other officers to bring women relatives aboard as passengers, and a good many appear to have extended the privilege to warrant officers and well-behaved seamen who requested it. When William Richardson was given permission to go ashore to say good-by to his wife before the *Tromp* sailed on a passage to the West Indies in 1800, he discovered that his wife "had fixed her mind to go with me, as it was reported the voyage would be short . . . I gave my consent, especially as the captain's the master's and boatswain's were going with them; the serjeant of marines and six other men's wives had leave to go." The boatswain also brought his daughter and the captain's wife her maid. Both the captain's wife and the master's were pregnant, and the captain's wife bore a son at sea. The master's wife, however, died of yellow fever.

In view of present-day concern about "problems relating to female sexuality," which many assume makes assigning women to combat ships unthinkable, there is something refreshing about the complacency with which the facts of life were faced in the great age of fighting sail, the period early in the nineteenth century when the British Navy fought for and maintained supremacy at sea over all other navies of the world.

The birth of a child was not normally recorded unless the child's mother was entitled to draw a ration, but occasionally an interesting occurrence would force the baby's presence on someone's attention. "This day the surgeon informed me that a woman on board had been labouring in childbirth for twelve hours," Captain W. N. Glascock recorded in an early nineteenth-century log, "and if I could see my way to permit the firing of a broadside to leeward, nature would be assisted by the shock. I complied with the request, and she was delivered of a fine male child." The spaces between the broadside guns were a preferred location for a woman in labor and gave rise to the saying "son of a gun."

Of course, that was inconvenient during battle. During action on "the Glorious First of June" in 1794, one of the proudest victories of the British Navy in the Napoleonic Wars, Mrs. Daniel McKenzie, of H.M.S. *Tremendous*, went into labor prematurely and delivered her son in the bread room. The infant was named Daniel Tremendous McKenzie. Four years later the birth of a child during another great victory, the Battle of the Nile, was laconically recorded by a sailor: "The women behaved as well as the men . . . There was some of the women wounded, and one woman belonging to Leith died of her wounds. One woman bore a son in the heat of the action; she belonged to Edinburgh."

What did women do on British warships besides have babies? Well, some worked as domestic servants with an official navy rating. It was a captain's privilege to appoint a certain number of "Captain's Servants," usually four per hundred of the ship's company, to sew, help with the laundry, and attend to other personal needs of the officers. Often these were children. The cabin boy might be a youngster being groomed for a career at sea, and other boys too immature to be appointed as midshipmen might serve as captain's servants until they had grown enough to be promoted.

The captain filled other vacancies for servants from the wives of the standing officers — the gunner, boatswain, carpenter, and perhaps the cook. As late as World War I, a woman was carried on a ship's books with the rating "Captain's Servant." Kathleen Dyer served for two and a half years aboard H.M.S. *Calypso*. "Owing to some foolish quibble on the part of the Admiralty," wrote a correspondent to the *Mariner's Mirror*, "Miss Dyer was refused the Naval War and Victory medals, though they were awarded to all other ranks and ratings serving in the ship during the period."

Such "quibbling" is found repeatedly in the history of women in the military services. For instance, Daniel Tremendous McKenzie was awarded the Naval General Service medal, with his rating recorded as "Baby," in recognition of his presence on the Glorious First of June, but the admiralty ruled against allowing the medal to any of the women, because it would leave the naval office "exposed to *innumerable* applications of the same nature."

When a ship saw action, all women aboard appear to have been put to useful work. Nancy Perriam, one of the few navy women to have left a written record, gives a rare glimpse into women's activity while the ship was under fire. She served with her husband aboard H.M.S. *Orion*, and her function was "to make and mend the captain's clothes." On February 14, 1797, she recalled, she had begun work on a flannel shirt when she heard the rumble of guns. Battle had been joined with a French ship off Cape St. Vincent. She immediately put down her sewing and began carrying gunpowder instead. When she was no longer needed at that post, she went down to the cockpit to help the surgeon. A year later, she followed the same pattern at the Battle of the Nile. A seaman at that battle who was assigned to a station below decks later stated, "I saw little of this action. Any information we got was from the boys and women who carried the powder . . . I was much indebted to the Gunner's wife, who gave her husband and me a drink of wine now and then, which lessened our fatigue much." As before, Nancy Perriam ended up in the cockpit. She especially remembered the bravery of a young midshipman, whose arm was taken out of its socket. "The boy bore the operations without a murmur," she wrote, "and when it was over turned to me and said, 'Have I not borne it like a man?' Having said this he immediately expired."

Carrying powder and nursing may have been the usual assignments of British navy women during battle, but some took a more active role. Admiral Rodney, it is said, once observed a woman serving with a gun crew on the main deck of his flagship. When asked what she was doing there, she explained that her husband had been wounded and sent down to the cockpit and she was taking his place. "Do you think, your honour," she added boldly, "I am afraid of the *French?*" The admiral decided to overlook the irregularity, if it was one, and gave the woman a gift of ten guineas.

When a woman served beyond the call of duty, a special gift was her only possible reward. Wives did not claim wages or a share of prize money, although they presumably enjoyed part of their husbands' share. Some peculiar methods were employed when it became necessary to pay a woman for her work. The strangest, perhaps, was to rate as an "Able Seaman" a woman who had been hired to serve as lady's maid to several princesses embarked as passengers. This was done by special order of Sir George Cockburn, a Lord of the Admiralty, to whom it seemed the easiest way out of the difficulty.

A problem also arose when a woman was widowed. Unlisted in the muster book, she could not draw rations in her own right. Captain Thomas Foley of the *Goliath* got around that great injustice after three seamen's wives and one marine's wife were widowed by suddenly adding their names to the muster book. From August 3 to November 30, 1798, Sarah Bates, Ann Taylor, Elizabeth Moore, and Mary French appear on the record for the first time, "victualled at two-thirds allowance, per Captain's order, in consideration of their assistance in dressing and attending on the wounded, being widows of men slain in fight with the enemy on 1st August, 1798." Their names were dropped from the list four months later, while the ship was still at sea, with the notation, "their further assistance not being required." Obviously, the ration had been intended as pay for services, not charity. Presumably the four were not tossed overboard after their official rationing stopped, and they must have been fed somehow. They were probably allowed to share with their husbands' former messmates, as they had done as wives.

A few other glimpses of women working on navy ships survive. A British official traveling aboard H.M.S. *Diamond Rock* in 1804–1805 helped pass the time at sea by sketching his surroundings. In one of his pictures, a woman, whose presence is nowhere else recorded, stands in the foreground feeding the livestock.

Admiral George Vernon Jackson remembered that when he was a midshipman serving aboard the *Lapwing* in 1801, the ship ran aground. "Whilst occupied in getting the ship off the Shoal," he recalled, "it was amusing to see how some women — forty or fifty in number — who were on board exerted themselves at the ropes." Another sea emergency focused a spotlight on otherwise invisible females. The *Horatio* ran onto a needle rock off Guernsey and began to leak badly. The captain headed for port, racing against the water rushing into the hold. Later he praised the ship's women, who "rendered essential service in thrumming the sail," that is, roughing up its surface and making it more absorbent by working in short bits of rope yarn. The sail was then lowered over the hole in the ship's bottom to slow the leak.

Of course, women were not always an asset during an emergency. James Gardner recalled the time a fire broke out aboard the *Orestes* when he was serving on her. The blaze began in the cabin directly above the powder magazine; candles had ignited the curtains. Before it was brought under control, the fire "occasioned the utmost terrors among the ship's company . . . It was ludicrous to see the captain with a speaking trumpet exerting himself to keep order, and the carpenter's wife catching him round the legs, and while he was calling for Water she was screaming out Fire."

The commander of the British Mediterranean fleet in 1796 was disturbed by what he felt was excessive consumption of water by women, and he threatened to enforce the rule against women going to sea if they continued to waste water on such nonessentials as washing. "There being reasons to apprehend that a number of women have been clandestinely brought from England to several ships . . . the respective Captains are required by the Admiral to admonish those ladies upon the waste of water, and other disorders committed by them, and to make known to all, that on the first proof of water being obtained for washing from the scuttle-butt or otherwise, under false pretenses, every woman in the fleet who has not been admitted under the authority of the Admiralty or the Commander-in-Chief, will be shipped for England by the first convoy."

A year later women were still doing their laundry and Admiral Jervis was still threatening. "It will become my indispensable duty to land all the women in the squadron at Gibraltar, unless this alarming evil is immediately corrected." A decade later women still sailed with the Mediterranean fleet.

Some women were regularly named in the supernu-

merary list of the muster books of British warships because they were a recognized part of the military estab-
lishment. The wives of soldiers, including soldiers
serving temporarily as marines, were entitled by law to
draw a two-thirds ration for themselves and a half ration
for each of their children when they traveled with their
husbands.

Sometimes, if ships sailed in convoy, the wives traveled together on a separate vessel. One such ship was
captured by the French off Gibraltar in 1782. An officer
recalling the engagement felt the English had come off
well enough, "with the baggage and the soldiers' wives,
the only loss sustained." Officers' wives also traveled in
separate ships on occasion; the Americans captured two
boatloads in the first three months of 1778.

Baroness Frederika von Riedesel, wife of the German
general who commanded the Hessians during the American Revolution, traveled to America in a merchant ship
specially hired for the purpose in a convoy guarded by
several men-of-war. She embarked on the *Blonde* with
her children and a number of servants and probably had
as pleasant a crossing as was possible for anyone in the
eighteenth century. She planned everything in advance,
being especially careful to have enough food taken aboard
because she had heard dreadful stories of ships running
so short of provisions that officers had to eat the same
rations as common soldiers or sailors. A good cook was
aboard, and the baroness recorded that "every day we
had four and often five and six dishes that were right
well prepared." Several of the ship's officers' families

were aboard, and the baroness shared her meals with them. She took the unavoidable hardships with good spirit. When seasickness struck the children and servants, she recruited a fifer and three drummers from among the soldiers aboard and had them all dance on the deck. There were storms when the "ship staggered so dreadfully" that she "often fell down," and it was frequently foggy and cold. But when the weather was calm, they paid visits to the other ships; and when the *Blonde* passed close to the *Henry*, which carried the German troops, the baroness accepted their cheers and held up the children for the troops to see. On the later trip home, aboard the *Little Seal* after the war was lost, the baroness still had her composure. She described an accident when part of the stern to which their private latrine was attached was torn away and sank. "This tore away our little Necessary," she wrote, "and it was very fortunate that no one was in it at the time."

The wives of ordinary soldiers were usually illiterate, and the conditions under which they traveled were far less comfortable, but they probably resembled the general's wife in a cheerful determination to make the best of it. And because their homes ashore were a corner of the army barracks screened off with a blanket and the food the same poor provisions allowed the men, they were used to roughing it. Yet officers, and other literate passengers, described the harsh conditions that an army in transport had to endure, often for many months. "It was always hot and in rough weather the stench was appalling," wrote a Royal Engineer subaltern of a voy-

age to India. "It was bad enough to pay a short visit to
the troop decks. To stay down there every night and all
night must have been hell. I pitied the rank and file,
but men were tough in those days." So were women.

Little is known about the exact arrangements aboard
transport ships before the end of the nineteenth century. It is unlikely that women and children had a
separate berthing area. A description written in 1890
declares, "The women on board had no privacy — all
sleeping in a sort of long room or cabin in bunks in two
tiers . . . There were very few bathrooms, all of them
on the upper deck, and these had to be shared by all
the officers and their wives. To reach the bathrooms we
had to walk through two or three inches of very dirty
water, as that deck — on which some horses were
stalled — was also being swabbed down." The common
soldiers and their families, however, had no bathing facilities. An observer on a troopship bound for China in
1841 wrote, "No one can picture the indescribable misery of the women and children . . . Dirty, haggard,
and wretchedly dressed, they looked like slaves let
loose." Nevertheless, this writer continued, "They had
considered themselves fortunate in the miserable privilege of being included in the percentage of six women
to every hundred men. Had they been left at home, they
and their children would probably have been in a state
of starvation."

Both officers and soldiers were discouraged from marrying. In the 1860s the standing orders of the 52nd Light
Infantry read, "The regiment cannot furnish employ-

ment for more than a few women, consequently any increase of numbers diminishes the means of existence of those already belonging to the regiment. The small quantity of accommodation in barracks, the difficulty of procuring lodgings, the frequency of moving, and inconveniences attending marches and embarkations, are to be urged as dissuasives against imprudent marriages."

When a British regiment was shipped overseas and the limit of six wives per hundred men was enforced, which women would be permitted to accompany their husbands was decided by lot. Those told they must stay behind did not always accept the verdict as final. In the confusion of getting under way, some women went aboard, taking their children, and attempted to conceal themselves until it was too late to put them ashore. They were usually caught.

Another method, employed by a soldier with the Rifle Brigade embarking for the Crimean War, was to help his woman cut her hair short, get her a uniform, and put her in the ranks as the troops were boarded. The rifleman's wife got to the top of the gangway before she was identified and put ashore. Nevertheless, she and her husband had the right idea; the surest way for an unauthorized woman to go to sea on a warship was in male disguise. Surprisingly large numbers did exactly that.

Evidence concerning disguised women who served aboard warships, either as sailors or marines, exists only for those who were somehow unmasked by someone who believed the discovery worth recording. Thus two categories of such women are beyond recovery for historians: those who sailed with the connivance of other sailors or officers — a stowaway wife or "pretty cabin boy" for the captain, whose presence was taken for granted and so never written about; and those who performed their duties at sea so well that no one who lived with them in the crowded dark forecastle ever became suspicious of them and who never had occasion in later life to reveal the secret themselves.

That a woman could live in close quarters with men without revealing her sex is hard for many people to believe. Nevertheless, there is clear evidence that numerous women did so successfully. Tall, muscular, small-breasted women who entered the service with beardless boys in their early teens seem to have required only the appropriate clothing and self-assurance to carry off the masquerade. Because so many escaped detection for years, it is a safe assumption that many others were never discovered. As the history of the pirate Mary Read suggests, even a woman with a full bosom could disguise her sex successfully. In the age of fighting sail, such women had careers at sea. One "William Brown," for instance, was able to prove eleven years of service aboard the *Queen Charlotte* to the satisfaction of authorities in 1815. "William Brown" was a black woman who for many years held the rating of "Captain of the Maintop" in a British warship, an assignment given only to the most skilled and agile sailors. Another woman — "Tom Bowling" — had to give her background when she was brought before an English magistrate for a petty crime. She had been a boatswain's mate aboard a man-of-war for over twenty years and was drawing a pension for her service.

When records show the discovery of a woman posing as a man, they usually announce that she was therefore discharged from the service. Certainly regulations forbade enlisting women as regular sailors. Indeed, one early record describes how a New York woman who enlisted as a seaman was punished, when her sex was discovered, by being dropped three times from the yard-arm and then being tarred and feathered. Yet occasional evidence of females being retained in the service after discovery, both in America and abroad, suggests that there was a certain tolerance for such seamen. We have, for instance, Nellie Bowden, whose rating on the ship's books changes abruptly from "Ship's Boy" to "Domestic" as the female first name is added. Another example is found in the record of a court-martial in which one of the witnesses was "a little female tar, Elizabeth Bowden, who has been on board the *Hazard* these eight months. She appeared in court in a long jacket and blue trousers."

One can imagine a situation in which a "sister" might be taken for granted in the "brotherhood" of sailors. If she had been aboard for a while, doing her work, proving herself a satisfactory messmate, the discovery that she was a female might be a matter of interest, but nothing one wanted to make a fuss about; an "incest taboo" would protect the sister from attracting any unwanted sexual attentions. The ways in which the sex of a female sailor was discovered — or even more significant, the occasions on which it was kept a secret — suggest a certain amount of deliberate blindness.

Perhaps the easiest discovery ever made was that of Jeanette Colin, who abandoned ship at Trafalgar, with the rest of the crew of the French ship *Achille* when the powder magazine was about to blow up. She went into the water stark naked, was pulled out by the British schooner *Pickle*, then transferred as a prisoner of war to the *Revenge*. Although the fighting was still going on, the introduction of a naked lady onto the deck of the *Revenge* naturally attracted some attention, and there was a good bit of scurrying around to make her decent again. The first lieutenant provided a needle and thread, the purser a clean shirt and a large silk handkerchief, someone else a bit of fancy sprigged muslin, which was booty from a Spanish prize, and others collected sheets and curtains from their cots. The chaplain donated a pair of shoes. Jeanette Colin then told her story, which was a typical one. When the French fleet sailed from Cadiz, she said, according to a sailor aboard the *Revenge* who heard her, "all the females were ordered to go on shore; she was married, and to quit her husband could not endure the thought; she was therefore resolved to share his glory or his death. No time was lost in carrying her plan into execution; for, having rigged herself out in a suit of sailor's clothes, thus disguised, she entered on board, and went in the same ship with him, as a seaman. In this state she remained, doing duty, during the engagement, when, whilst fighting by the side of her husband, a ball killed him on the spot." As a widow, she had no further reason to remain a sailor and gratefully accepted passage to Gibraltar on the English ship. The number of women in male dress who were serving aboard the *Achille* when she went down will never be known; one other was picked up by the *Britannia*.

It seems clear that most women who volunteered for service aboard a warship did it because of a man. Indeed, the pattern was frequent enough to have become a standard theme of folk songs. In some verses, the woman did not consult with her lover before she

> *Put on a jolly sailor's dress*
> *And daubed her hands with tar*
> *To cross the raging sea*
> *On board a man-of-war.*

Sometimes, both in story and in fact, the man was not pleased to find his lady love at his side. Women might follow a man not only for love, but also out of hate. Deserted wives and lovers, determined to have their rights from a man known to have enlisted on a warship or in a regiment being shipped abroad, would contrive to take passage in the same way. A woman too poor to pay her traveling expenses might find this the most practical method.

Some women wronged by a man drifted into a permanent career at sea. This appears to be the case with Mary Anne Talbot, who published a long and detailed memoir of her life. Like all old sailors' reminiscences, it must be taken with a grain of salt, but there is sup-

porting evidence for most of the main details. She first
went to sea in male clothing in 1792 as a servant to an
officer whose regiment had been ordered to the West
Indies. Later, when the regiment was ordered to Flanders, she served under the officer as a drummer. She
later claimed that her service was against her will, that
the officer was a villain who had seduced her and kept
her with him by force. In any event, she deserted from
the regiment in 1793, disguised herself as a sailor, and
enlisted on a French ship that turned out to be a privateer. Talbot served as a regular member of the crew, but
because she refused to fight against her own people, she
said, she was severely beaten.

Eventually the privateer was taken by the English
warship *Queen Charlotte*. Talbot convinced the admiral
that she was on the privateer innocently and so was sent
aboard the *Brunswick*, where she carried powder for the
guns and was eventually promoted to principal cabin
boy. On the *Brunswick* she was wounded in action in
the Glorious First of June — grapeshot breaking the
bone near her ankle and lodging in the thigh just above
her knee. Although she was treated for these injuries by
the surgeon in the cockpit and later in a hospital ashore,
when she was healed she enlisted as a midshipman on
board the *Vesuvius*. Either the doctors had not discovered her sex or they did not care. Once in her career
she deliberately revealed her sex, after she was seized by
a press gang and preferred not to embark. She eventually retired from the sea, collecting a pension of twenty

pounds a year. She joined a theater company for a while, performing male and female roles.

Avoiding a press gang was the motivation for another woman to interrupt a naval career by voluntarily confessing her sex. In 1759 a woman aged about twenty and dressed in sailors' clothing was seized by the press in Plymouth. When she was put with other forced recruits into the town jail to prevent her escape, she confessed to being female. Her name was Hannah Whitney, she told the authorities, and she had been serving aboard British warships for five years. They would never have discovered her sex, she told them smugly, if they had not put her in a common jail. The press, then, was forced to release her. Whether she reenlisted at some time and place of her own choosing is unknown.

Perhaps the most incredible story of concealment, in which the woman revealed her sex only when she applied for a pension, is that of Hannah Snell. She enlisted in military service to find the husband who had left her penniless and pregnant. The child died soon after birth, and in 1743 "James Gray" enlisted in the army. Military discipline was severe in those days, and when charged by a sergeant with neglect of duty, the new recruit was sentenced to receive six hundred lashes. Did anyone notice anything unusual about "James Gray" when the recent mother was stripped to the waist for punishment? If so, it made very little difference; the officers interceded, but only after "James Gray" had taken five hundred lashes. At this point, however, Hannah Snell

deserted; a month later she signed up with a regiment
of marines.

The regiment embarked aboard the *Swallow*, and here
her work seemed to give satisfaction. The officers were
pleased at the new private's skill at washing, mending,
and cooking, and they also praised her courage when
the marines saw action. At the siege of Pondicherry,
Hannah Snell was one of the first invasion group that
crossed the river, with water chest-deep, under fire from
French batteries. She was on guard duty in the picket
ground for seven nights in succession, and then spent
two weeks in the trenches. Eventually she was put out
of action by wounds — six bullets in her right leg, five
in the left, and one in her abdomen. Once again, one
wonders about military surgeons, for it appears that Snell
kept the abdominal wound secret from them, allowing
only her legs to be treated, and took care of the most
serious injury herself with the help of a black woman of
the army to whom she confessed her sex.

After a stay in the hospital, she was assigned to the
Tartar Pink, where she performed the duties of a sailor,
and then to the *Eltham*. Aboard the latter she ran into
trouble again when she was suspected of stealing a shirt;
she spent five days confined in irons and then was given
five lashes. Otherwise, she got on well with her shipmates. They teased her a bit about not having a beard,
calling her "Miss Molly Gray," but they were soon convinced she was a regular guy, and "James Gray" became
known aboard as "Hearty Jemmy."

Hannah Snell retired from the sea in 1750 and her

history soon became common knowledge. As Mary Anne Talbot would do later, Snell supplemented a government pension by going on the stage. She had a good singing voice and was engaged to play the roles of various military and naval heroes, and to perform the manual and platoon exercises with a musket for the amusement of landlubbers who had never before seen a female marine. Later she found a still easier way to capitalize on her notoriety by opening a tavern. The signboard carried a portrait of her in uniform, under which was inscribed, "The Widow in Masquerade, or the Female Warrior."

The history of the United States Navy does not begin until the last decades of the eighteenth century. Sea warfare during the War for American Independence was mostly in the hands of America's allies, France and Spain, or of privateers, like John Paul Jones, and hastily assembled state navies.

American seafarers, however, drew from the British traditions, and the sporadic appearance of women on fighting ships continues in the naval history of the new nation. There were women aboard the galleys of the Pennsylvania Navy in 1776; we know because they were treated for "the itch" by a Quaker woman in New Jersey. And we know that Mary Pricely served as a nurse aboard the Maryland Navy's ship *Defence* during 1777 because she was paid for her services by the Maryland Council of Safety, although, as was customary, her name does not appear on the ship's muster roll. And we know that John Paul Jones sailed with a woman aboard at least

once — when he captured the *Drake* and his prisoners
included the cook's wife.

Nevertheless, American naval practices came to di-
verge from those of the British. The most important difference was that the United States did not use force to
recruit sailors for military service. Therefore, sailors
could be allowed shore leave and there was no need for
the system of shipboard prostitution that was so noto-
rious a part of life on a British man-of-war in port. That
is not to say that there were no prostitutes in American
ports. A sailor arriving in New York aboard the *Ontario*
in 1817 wrote, "Scarcely had our anchor gone from the
bow, before the ship was surrounded by land sharks and
bad women; the latter, however, were not permitted to
come aboard." Sailors who were not overly inhibited by
moral scruples could visit the bad women during liberty
hours. More significant, sailors who wanted to indulge
in the deeper pleasures of holy matrimony could visit
their homes and children. Since the United States did
not maintain fleets on distant stations, visits home were,
if not frequent, at least less infrequent than those of
British sailors. Furthermore, an American Navy man
need not fear that he would be immediately posted to a
new ship every time he reached port, without any chance
to visit home. Finally, if a sailor wanted family life, he
was free, in the United States, to leave the navy after
his tour and enlist on a fishing vessel that was at sea for
shorter periods. If he could accumulate enough capital,
he could even become master of his own ship and take
his family along when he went to sea.

Officers and petty and warrant officers in the American Navy continued to follow the British traditions governing wives at sea. When a squadron of warships was sent to the Mediterranean in 1803, Commodore Richard Valentine Morris, aboard the frigate *Chesapeake*, was accompanied by his wife, an infant son, and a black lady's maid. The regulations stated — echoing those of Great Britain — that no woman could go to sea without the permission of the Navy Department or the commander of the squadron. As commodore, Morris obviously felt entitled to grant such permission. Nor was he stingy with it, for he allowed other men to bring their wives aboard. While cruising the Mediterranean, the wife of James Low, captain of the forecastle, went into labor. The familiar home remedy was applied: *Chesapeake* fired a broadside, and into the world came a new little son-of-a-gun. One of the midshipmen, Melancthon Taylor Woolsey, was asked to stand as godfather, and the baby was named for him. In return, the midshipman arranged for a "handsome collation of wine & Fruit" to follow the infant's christening. The new mother was unwell, so the wife of the gunner, Mrs. Hayes, stood in for her. This signal honor for Mrs. Hayes suddenly brought a few other women into the glare of the historical record, for Midshipman Henry Wadsworth recorded in his journal, "The other Ladies of the Bay — The Forward most part of the Birth Deck [*sic*] — viz. Mrs. Watson: the Boatswain's wife, Mrs. Myres the Carpenter's Lady — with Mrs. Crosby the corporal's lady; got drunk in their own Quarters out of pure spite — not being invited to celebrate the Christening of Melancthon Woolsey Low."

During the next two decades, several courts-martial arose from the presence of women aboard American Navy ships. In each case the woman's bad character was more at issue than her gender. One has the distinct impression that if they had not made enemies aboard nobody would have said anything about their presence. The first case was initiated by a letter to the Navy Department, from the master's mate of a gunboat commanded by Lieutenant John B. Nicholson, complaining about the woman Nicholson had taken aboard at Norfolk. "We are all hands liked to famished to death for want of water on the passage [to Cuba] in consequence of her having expended about one gallon per day washing her face and hands three or four times per day," he wrote. It was not safe to complain to the captain about this female; she was able to use her influence to have men flogged and disrated and did so. "There was never peace nor quietness after she came on board," the mate told the gentlemen of the Navy Department, "and I expect that I shall have to quit the navy in consequence of her which I must say I am very sorry of it, and I think the gun boats have come to a very high pitch when they are commanded by Common Prostitutes . . ." Lieutenant Nicholson was tried in November 1809 and found guilty of "absolutely unmorally and Scandalously Keeping a prostitute of the vilest class on board his vessel to the destruction of discipline and the dishonor of an officer." Nicholson was cashiered.

Meanwhile, two midshipmen, Thomas C. Magruder and William Peters, who commanded gunboats, had also taken female companions aboard. They went unnoticed by higher authority until the following spring, when Commodore David Porter received an anonymous letter. What seems to have disturbed Porter most was the charge that the midshipmen had cruelly mistreated the crew "at the instigation of the said prostitute." The court-martial on these cases found that charge not proved, and, indeed, concluded that the chief witness, Purser Steward Berryman, was guilty of perjury and sentenced him to be confined in wrist irons aboard Peters's vessel for thirty-nine days. The mere presence of prostitutes was a trivial matter; the midshipmen got off with a reprimand. The defense offered by Midshipman Peters suggests the attitudes of the time. Avoiding the central issue, namely, the unsavory reputation of his female guest, Peters argued to the court that "occasional indulgence in dalliance with the fair sex need not necessarily be construed as harming the interests of the Navy or demoralizing its men." And, "as to keeping a woman on board the vessel . . . he urges in excuse or justification *Example & Precedent,* of those superior in rank and older in service."

The next officer to get into trouble because of a female aboard his ship was Midshipman Robert N. Nichols, whose offense was marrying the woman. Nichols had taken one Hannah Damewood aboard a vessel in the Lake Ontario Squadron commanded by Captain M. T. Woolsey. Woolsey knew Miss Damewood; she had been a servant in his home, and he had fired her because she was "lazy and filthy and supposed to be dishonest." Nichols claimed that he had first asked her aboard to nurse him when he was ill; the court of inquiry did not find reason to question that statement or to believe that Nichols had violated Captain Woolsey's standing order in bringing her aboard the ship. But after recovering from his illness, Nichols had gone before a justice of the peace and married the woman who had been considered unfit to serve as a servant in the captain's home. In doing so, "he has disgraced himself as an officer and a gentleman by his alliance, destroyed his reputation, and placed an unmoveable stigma on his character." That, however, was not grounds for either a court-martial or a divorce; and perhaps the shipboard nurse who had won an honest proposal of marriage did not deserve the bad reputation the captain gave her.

Because American seamen were not forced into military service and American soldiers were not sent overseas, there was far less motive for women to disguise themselves as men to join the navy. Yet there is a memoir, dating from the War of 1812, of a woman who went to sea as a United States marine aboard the U.S.S. *Constitution*. Unlike the memoirs of Mary Anne Talbot and Hannah Snell, *The Female Marine, or Adventures of Miss Lucy Brewer* was published under a pseudonym. "Miss Brewer" carefully disguised her real identity to protect her family, not so much from the knowledge that they had had a daughter in the marines, which should be nothing to be ashamed of, but from the knowledge that she joined the marines to escape from a house of prostitution. Because of her desire for anonymity it has been impossible to find evidence definitely confirming — or refuting — the statements presented in the book. "Miss Lucy Brewer" never applied for a government pension, but she must have made a tidy sum from the sale of her book, which went into several printings.

Someone else may have made money too, for another pamphlet, published by Rachel Sperry, adds some details to the Brewer story. Its legitimacy, however, is also impossible to determine. Mrs. Sperry was the proprietor of Lucy Brewer's brothel. She had never been told the real name of the pregnant sixteen-year-old she had taken in, but she immediately recognized both "Lucy" and herself when she read a copy of *The Female Marine* and wrote her own pamphlet to defend her reputation.

The Brewer story is a lively one. Pregnant and deserted by her lover, Lucy had walked forty miles from her home in a Massachusetts town to Boston rather than disgrace her parents. She claimed Mrs. Sperry tricked her; Mrs. Sperry said Lucy knew exactly what she was doing when she accepted an offer of employment. At any rate, after her baby was born — and soon died — she was one of the "naughty ladies" in Mrs. Sperry's stable. There she met a young lieutenant from the *Constitution* who suggested to her that by dressing in men's clothing she could leave Mrs. Sperry's house without fear of prosecution or jail and that the disguise would also give her the freedom to travel and find adventure. He told her about Deborah Sampson, whose experiences in the army during the American Revolution, disguised as a male, were described in the popular book *The Female Review*. "From this moment," Brewer wrote, "I became dissatisfied with my situation in life . . . I felt now no other disposition than in disguise to visit other parts of the country, and to pursue a course of life less immoral and destructive to my peace and happiness in this life."

Brewer describes how she bought sailors' clothing, bandaged her breasts, and put on a pair of tight underpants. Thus disguised she presented herself as a new recruit, avoiding a physical examination by an "artful stratagem." The stratagem, according to Mrs. Sperry, was the direct intervention of the lieutenant, who introduced the prospective marine as his cousin. Rank had its privileges, and Lucy Brewer was enlisted. In fact, there may have been connivance in enabling the lieutenant to smuggle a woman aboard. Women were not supposed to be recruited, but then neither were free black men, and the *Constitution* carried a number of black sailors whose courage was commended in official reports. Regulations should never be confused with reality.

Brewer went aboard ignorant of the use of firearms, but, as was the custom, new recruits were drilled on the deck and, she wrote, "I soon learnt to load and discharge with an expertness not surpassed by any in my corps." Perhaps not much expertness was required. It was common for as many as half the marines aboard a warship to be young recruits, and few were apt to be experienced marksmen.

Brewer first saw action after only seventeen days at sea, when the *Constitution* engaged the British frigate *Guerriere*. Brewer described her feelings before battle: "I felt an extreme desire to render myself conspicuous, and to perform that which woman never before achieved." Most of Brewer's descriptions of engagements, like those of other sailors polishing up their memoirs for publication, contain little that is not in the newspaper accounts. She describes the battle with the *Guerriere* and another famous battle with the *Java*. On life below decks, she is silent; perhaps she maintained her friendship with the lieutenant. At any rate, there was certainly never any official record of a female being aboard the *Constitution* during the three years Brewer claimed to have been on active duty. The secret was kept very well.

After the War of 1812, the unofficial practice of taking wives to sea continued. The record of their presence, when it exists, is almost always in private papers, not official records, so it is impossible to say exactly when the last wife embarked with a navy ship on active duty. Susan Dillwyn Conner, the wife of Captain David Conner, was with him when the sloop-of-war *John Adams* sailed to the Mediterranean in 1834; we know because she kept a journal, which is preserved in the Philadelphia Maritime Museum. As late as 1910, Harriet D. Welles accompanied her husband on a tour of duty aboard the U.S.S. *New Orleans*. The journal she kept is preserved in the Library of Congress and records her impressions of navy life and the sights she saw in Shanghai, Yokahama, Chuzenjui, Hong Kong, and Manila. Women who enlisted in the navy disguised as men also continue to appear occasionally into the present century. For instance, in March 1907, John Wilkinson, a sailor aboard the American battleship *Vermont*, was discovered to be a female while "he" was taking a bath.

Although their numbers declined as the nineteenth century progressed, women taken to sea aboard navy ships attained a new high in status as contributing members of their companies during the Civil War. Indeed, during that war, a woman briefly commanded an American warship. Her tenure was irregular, unofficial, unrecognized, and unrewarded; nevertheless, it was definitely a success. The woman was the wife of a warrant officer aboard the Federal brigantine *J. P. Ellicott*, which was captured by the Confederate privateer *Retribution* in 1863. The officers and men were all taken aboard the Southern vessel, while a prize crew was put aboard the *J. P. Ellicott*. No one bothered about the woman, presuming a female to be harmless, and she was left to putter around the galley and serve refreshments. Exploiting the enemy's weaknesses, the woman got the entire prize crew drunk. This should not have been possible. A year earlier, Congress had passed a law stating, "On September 1, 1862, the spirit ration shall forever cease and thereafter no distilled spirituous liquor shall be admitted on board vessels of war." Neither liquor nor a woman should have been aboard a United States Navy ship, but in this case it was fortunate that both were. When the Confederates were suitably inebriated, the Yankee woman secured them all below deck, took over the vessel single-handedly, and piloted it into the harbor at St. Thomas, where she surrendered her prisoners — and her command.

What was new during the Civil War, however, was not female courage, ingenuity, or seamanship, for these had frequently been displayed before. The novelty was the acceptance aboard navy ships of women who were neither wives whose work was taken for granted nor females disguised as men, but merely people with a job to do.

The first women to board a commissioned vessel of the U.S. Navy with a job description unrelated to marital status were four members of the Sisters of the Holy Cross and five black women: Sisters Veronica, Calista, Adela, and St. John of the Cross, assisted by Alice Kennedy, Sarah Kinno, Ellen Campbell, Betsy Young, and Dennis Downs. The first of them boarded the hospital ship U.S.S. *Red Rover* on Christmas Eve 1862, and although it would be nearly half a century before Congress recognized the existence of a Navy Nurse Corps, these nine women were, in effect, its founders. Other women served aboard civilian ships operating as floating hospitals during the war, and since 1730 "washerwomen" had been aboard hospital ships commissioned by the British Navy. But the washerwomen were equivalent to captain's servants, that is, chosen from wives of

the crew, and the women who served aboard Sanitary
Commission hospital ships were clearly civilians. The
status of the women aboard the U.S.S. *Red Rover* was
rather different.

The Sisters of the Holy Cross were not a nursing order. They were no better trained in giving medical care
than the average American woman of the time; they
learned after they were assigned to the work. What made
them valuable as military nurses was that they were part
of a disciplined corps that understood military discipline
and the chain of command. Until the navy was ready to
integrate women workers into its own hierarchy, some
such substitute was needed to avoid anarchy.

The U.S.S. *Red Rover* was the first hospital ship ever
commissioned by the American Navy. Originally built
as a barge to carry ice, it was refitted at the time it was
restaffed. In addition to a huge icebox, it had bathrooms, a laundry, and an elevator to move patients from
lower-deck berths to the operating room on the top deck.
This was far more comfortable for both patients and
medical personnel than making do in the cockpit, as was
necessary in the days when warships were the only navy
ships and had to be self-sustaining, operating without
auxiliaries.

It took many years for women serving on hospital
ships to be recognized as military personnel. Today they
are taken for granted. Indeed, the contemporary ban on
women serving aboard "combat" vessels in the navy
specifically excludes nurses.

When North fought South in the War Between the

States, there was relatively little action on the high seas. Yet each side attempted to blockade the ports of the other and captured civilian prizes far from home. Women engaged in respectable businesses, whaling or commerce, might find themselves taken as prisoners of war because their vessel was registered in an "enemy" state. They did not take kindly to having their lives disrupted by what some of them viewed as the childishness of male naval officers. Mrs. Nichols, wife of the captain of a Maine merchant vessel, *Delphine*, was clearly in a fury when she was forced to transfer herself, her six-year-old son, the steward's wife, and all of their baggage aboard the Confederate cruiser *Shenandoah*, which had "captured" the unarmed *Delphine* in the middle of the Indian Ocean. "Young man," she said severely to the Confederate captain as soon as she was on deck, "you should be ashamed of yourself, going around sinking ships and barks belonging to honest folk. What would your mother say?"

To Mrs. Nichols, freedom of the seas was the most important of all political principles. The concerns of land were remote from her life on the ocean. Even in wartime, seafaring families of the nineteenth century lived in a world apart. They are the subject of the next two chapters.

4

Whalers

THE PETROLEUM INDUSTRY today is what the whaling industry was in the nineteenth century. Before the discovery of oil in the ground, oil from whales was used to lubricate the wheels of machinery and to fuel lamps. And as petroleum is used now to make plastics and many clothing materials, whalebone was used in the nineteenth century for a multitude of practical and decorative household items and as an essential part of women's wardrobes in the days when fashion demanded corsets and hoop skirts.

Americans dominated the whaling industry from its beginnings in the late seventeenth century, and whaling reached its peak in the years just before the Civil War. After the war, for a variety of reasons, it began to decline, and by the end of the century American whalers had virtually disappeared. Today, as mechanized whaling vessels pursue a dwindling number of animals, some Americans are going to sea again in private efforts to save the planet's largest mammals from extinction. From the beginning, women have been part of the whaling story.

The first whaling operations were shore-based. On Long Island and Nantucket, lookouts scanned the water, watching for whales. When one was spotted, small boats would push off from the beach and give chase. In these early days, the whalers' prey was the species known as the right whale. After a few decades of shore-based hunting, right whales became scarce.

Then New Englanders went farther out to sea in larger craft, trailing their whaleboats behind them. There they discovered a new kind of whale, the sperm whale, larger — and more valuable — than the right whale. Almost overnight, whaling became a major industry. One of the first people to go into the business of hunting whales at sea was Martha Smith, who owned an entire fleet of ships by 1718. Many other women invested in whalers during the following century; indeed such investment eventually became the most popular form for widows of whalers and fishermen from such places as Nantucket, Martha's Vineyard, and New Bedford. During the eighteenth century, women remained on shore and did not follow the whaling men to sea, but in the nineteenth century that changed.

As more and more ships hunted whales to satisfy a growing market for whale oil and bone, voyages grew longer and longer. Rather than spend a morning rowing a boat from the beach, nineteenth-century whalemen took vessels around the world and into all latitudes on hunts that lasted not for hours but for years. A navy wife left on shore in the nineteenth century might easily go for months without hearing from her husband, and the wife of a merchant seaman might expect a separation of a year or more. But a whaler's wife, in the nineteenth century, endured such extended separations and had such undependable means of communication that for all practical purposes she might as well have been a widow. Voyages three to five years long were common, and once home, a whaling man stopped barely long enough to be introduced to his youngest child before he was off to sea again. The risks of whaling and temptations to desert in some warm Pacific isle were such that odds were two to one against any individual sailor returning from a voyage. The railed platforms built on the rooftops in whaling ports were used by women to scan the horizon hoping for a sign of a returning ship, and so came to be known as "widows' walks." This was an unnatural, unpleasant life for both husbands and wives. Sweethearts and young married couples might endure a separation or two, but as families grew and the man prospered enough to become master of his own ship, the sacrifice of a normal family life became increasingly difficult to accept. The solution was obvious: take the family and make a home at sea.

The first family to make a home on a whaling ship was the Russells of Nantucket. In 1817 Mary Russell joined her husband Laban aboard the *Hydra*, and their twelve-year-old son William was signed on as cabin boy.

The voyage was so successful that the family made another in 1823 aboard the *Emily*. William was by then a qualified harpooner, but his seven-year-old brother Charles went along too, as his mother did, simply to keep the family together. A decade later, whaling wives were common, and before the Civil War hundreds of New England women who had never seen Boston or New York City were familiar with exotic ports throughout the Pacific.

Today most people's knowledge of whaling probably comes from Herman Melville's epic novel *Moby Dick*. Captain Ahab had no women with him, and those who think of whaling in terms of Ahab's mad quest for the killer white whale must surely be startled by the far more typical picture of whaling life left in old letters and journals by seafaring women. Here we find a world of self-satisfied Victorian domesticity, complete with ladies seated on horsehair sofas embroidering elaborate quilts and little girls practicing their scales on a parlor organ. Melville wrote in another of his novels, *White Jacket*, that a ship "is but this old-fashioned world of ours afloat." Certainly the whaling wives did their best to make that true aboard the ships that were, in every sense, their homes. Their journals tell of lives dominated by washing, sewing, caring for the children, training servants, and making visits, as though the transfer of such feminine preoccupations to the high seas was the most natural thing in the world. And perhaps it was. The challenges they faced, though real enough, were surely no greater than those faced by women determined to make a "proper" home in a covered wagon crossing Indian country or in a sodhut on an isolated prairie.

Keeping a journal was a peculiarly feminine pastime in the nineteenth century, and these manuscript volumes are a treasure for all historians of women's history. The books whalers' wives filled at sea preserve a picture of daily life with a vividness missing from the logs kept by their captain husbands and rarely found in writings of the frequently illiterate officers and almost always illiterate crew. The captain's log was usually confined to observations on weather and whales and ships sighted. Otherwise only extraordinary events were noted, and the activities of the females aboard were rarely in that category. Thus Captain Valentine Lewis began his journal of the voyage of *Corinthian* in 1866 with these words: "At 9 A.M. all hands came on board and made all sail and went to sea with 32 men and wone Lady all told." The "wone Lady" was his wife, Ethelinda, who is mentioned only once again, when she fell and hurt her hand a year and a half later. Contrast the entry made by Eliza Williams on her first day at sea in 1858: "Now I am in the place that is to be my home, posibly [*sic*] for 3 or 4 years; but I can not make it appear to me so yet it all seems so strange, so many Men and not one Woman beside myself; the little Cabin that is to be all my own is quite pretty; as well as I can wish, or expect on board of a Ship. I have a rose geranium to pet . . . and I see there is a kitten on board."

Although we cannot tell about Ethelinda, it is clear

that Eliza expected to enjoy life as the one lady aboard.

Women who did not go to sea often assumed that a wife who did was accepting a life of great hardship and tended to pity her. Such confined quarters! Such great isolation! And those horrible storms! Whaling wives tended to be impatient with such talk. Charlotte Hillman Reynolds, who spent nearly a decade at sea, vigorously denied that it was a hard life. "Not at all," she would say. "We had a happy time. Once in the *James Arnold* we went through a bad hurricane off Hatteras — the guard rails were awash with the seas, but there are just as severe storms ashore, I have learned. Things were very nice for me aboard. I used to have my organ, and on one ship I had a bathroom." She always insisted that her seafaring years were the happiest time of her life.

The motion of the ship, particularly during bad weather, took some getting used to, but eventually a gale became just a passing event — not pleasant, of course, but nothing to have hysterics over. Eliza Williams was nearly eight months pregnant when the *Florida* first encountered a prolonged period of rough weather. "I don't like it at all," she wrote. "I can't go around like the Sailors, as I can in a smooth day." After the baby was born she still did not quite have her sea legs. "The swell makes the Ship roll and that is not very pleasant, though I have got very well used to it now, except when I start for some place in a hurry and get there quicker than I want to. But I think I shall practice caution now for the Baby's sake."

Mary Lawrence, who was at sea aboard the ship *Ad-*

dison in another part of the world at the same time Eliza Williams was learning to walk the deck with an infant in her arms, had been out a year and took everything in stride. Waking during a gale one night, she wrote, "My first thought was that the ship was going down, but my fears were entirely groundless, as we only shipped a heavy sea which broke one of the skylights and sent the water into the after cabin. The steward was called up to bail it out, which he soon did." Her only complaint was that "almost everything was wet through."

An occasional wetting, however, was no great matter. Like the rolling and pitching of the ship, it was something one adjusted to and took with good humor. After another gale, Mary Lawrence observed, "I could go out to my meals today without fear of my dinner being thrown in my lap or under the table. For several days past we have been under the necessity of holding on our mugs with one hand and our plates with the other and occasionally snatching a mouthful between the rolls. Some very amusing scenes are enacted often at the table in a gale of wind. The sauce will somehow get on our meat, and the gravy in its turn will get upon the pudding."

Mary Lawrence's good appetite during a storm indicates that she had overcome the misery known as seasickness, of which most people experienced at least a touch when they first went to sea. Some women suffered from it severely and might even have had to abandon their plans to live with their husbands as a result. Captain Horatio N. Gray of the *Cossack* wrote, "My poor

Emma is suffering much from her old enemy seasickness and there seems to be no cure for her. Whiskey
gives some relief, as does Brandy and water — but it is
only temporary. I am very sorry that I ever gave my
consent to her coming on this voyage." Most women,
however, soon got over their queasiness. Homesickness
was apt to be a more persistent discomfort.

There seemed to be no help for it. Wives who stayed
at home missed their husbands, and those who went to
sea missed the family and friends they left behind. That
was especially true when younger children had to be left
to attend school. It would have been much easier to endure had there been a reliable means of communication
with those at home, but there was not. Letters were
placed aboard ships met at sea, and these would be
traded back and forth as ships passed each other until
eventually they reached a vessel heading toward the
home port.

Mary Lawrence was unable to send any letters home
from *Addison* on her first cruise until the ship had been
out more than six weeks. "I know my mother, at least,
feels very anxious," she wrote in her journal. Letters
coming from home were even less certain of reaching a
destination. It took two years for a box sent by Mary
Lawrence's mother to reach her, and one whaling wife
recalled that of more than a hundred letters she wrote
to her husband while he was at sea on a three-year voyage, he received only six. The difficulty was that letters
could not be addressed to a fixed location — only to a
ship. And the ship might be anywhere in the world;

captains regularly changed their original sailing plans if hunting looked more promising somewhere else. Ships that met at sea passed on gossip of the other ships they had seen and exchanged letters and parcels accordingly. But there was no certainty of meeting any given ship; if ships passed just beyond each other's sight, the messages from home would pass by too. A letter from home that reached a whaler in less than six months was considered to be very promptly delivered.

Some women seemed unable to keep their thoughts from drifting toward those left behind, worrying in particular about those who might be sick or dead. Even the sturdiest minds could not help, at times, longing for the old familiar places. "How I wish I could enjoy this month at home, by far the most pleasant of the year to me," wrote Mary Lawrence on June 1, 1858, as the *Addison*, surrounded by fog and ice in the Bering Sea near the coast of Siberia, hunted whales. "Our little village at this time presents a delightful appearance to my imagination . . . The trees . . . have adorned themselves with new foliage, while the whole air is fragrant with flowers and redolent with the songs of the birds." Eliza Williams also longed for New England in the spring and wished for home on Christmas Eve and on the day when one of the two sons she had left behind was celebrating his fifth birthday.

In moderation, thoughts of home were not harmful. Eliza Williams understood this well and stopped herself when her ruminations took a depressing turn. "That dear word home; how many tender associations are connected with that one word and center about the heart, causing it to throb every time it is brought to mind . . . But I will drop the subject; it is too gloomy to contemplate, and return to the Ship."

Lucy Smith embarked, in October 1869, on the ship *Nautilus*, certain she was making the right decision in deciding to accompany her husband. Two weeks later she recorded in her journal, "Although I have been seasick I have not yet been homesick, nor have I even for a moment thought I would wish my husband to be here without me." But by Christmas she was depressed: "Christmas is nearly gone and it has not been a very merry one to me, for I have felt unusually sad this afternoon. As I look forward there seems to be so little on earth to live for." Only her son Freddie, who was with her on the *Nautilus*, gave her a reason to go on. A month later Freddie celebrated his fourth birthday. "Four years this morn since Freddie first saw the light . . . Little did I then think that four years from that day would find us on the wide ocean but it is so." In March her mood was still low: "Another Sabbath is numbered with those gone before," she wrote on Sunday the thirteenth, "one less to spend on Earth, one day nearer our Eternal home."

Only one thing could be more depressing than life on the *Nautilus*, and that was life anywhere else. On July 5, 1870, Lucy Smith recalled, "It is one year today since my beloved husband returned from a four years' voyage. Oh! how glad I am that I can be with him this voyage instead of being left at home, and hope he will never go another voyage without me." It was May 1874 before the Smiths returned to New England. "Although many times life on board has not been particularly pleasant," Lucy Smith wrote on their last night aboard the *Nautilus*, ". . . it is with feelings of pleasure not unmingled with pain that I shall bid her adieu. She has borne us safely thousands of miles and for more than four and a half years has been our home."

Perhaps the greatest threat to happiness at sea was boredom. Of course, people generally make their own happiness or misery, and people who were bored on the whalers probably would not have been any happier on a farm many miles from neighbors or stores. Those blessed with the ability to live in the moment and appreciate the small things that passed before their eyes found life at sea beautiful and satisfying. On her first Thanksgiving away from home, Mary Lawrence missed "Grandma's nice turkey," but had no wish to be on land when she could watch the waves as the *Addison* plowed through heavy seas. "It sometimes seems impossible that we can live through it," she wrote, "but our gallant ship rides along fearlessly. It is grand beyond anything I ever witnessed, sublimity itself." A week later the sea was calm, and Mary Lawrence "went on deck immediately after breakfast to view old Ocean in another aspect. Everything is smiling and serene; one would never suspect the treachery that lurks in his bosom. Everything seems changed. This is one of the most delightful moments of my life. I do not wonder that so many choose a sailor's life. It is a life of hardship, but it is a life full of romance and interest."

It seems that every woman who went whaling quickly began to collect "curiosities" to help her remember the wonderful things she was seeing. In later years these became prized possessions. The niece of Phebe Ann Pease, who had sailed on the *Cambria*, said her aunt so treasured the mementos of her whaling days that she would never light the wood stove in her parlor for fear that ashes might fall on her treasures.

Eliza Williams took her first prize when she had been at sea about a month and a flying fish flew on board. "It was a beuty," she wrote in her journal, "about the size of a sucker, quite hansome spots on it of dark and light brown, but the wings were beutiful; it had the appearance of a thin skin with devitions of some kind of a hard sinewey substance that they could close them together when not flying. They fly up out of the water, and skim along quite a long way, and then dart under. I have one of the wings pressed."

In her early months at sea Mary Lawrence recorded saving a bone after having albacore for breakfast and putting a crab leg in her workbox. She was also fascinated when sailors out after a whale "brought home a curiosity in one of the boats, a piece of kelp or seaweed (called here a sea serpent) very much in the shape of a serpent, forty-six feet in length." Her husband had it preserved for her.

Women added to their collections of curiosities on

shopping trips ashore and by receiving gifts when visiting aboard other ships. Despite long weeks or even months at sea without seeing another ship, a whale, or so much as a bird, these periods of relative monotony were broken by stops at exotic places as far from the lives of most American women of the nineteenth century as the moon and the planets. Whaling wives went to places no white woman had ever visited before and saw such things as naked men tattooed from head to foot and cannibal queens who, it was said, might take a bite out of their own arms when they wanted to emphasize a point in conversation. "When I was a school-girl studying geography," Mary Lawrence wrote, "how strange it would have seemed had anyone told me that I should view these places with my own eyes." Children studying astronomy today may have such feelings a few years from now as space exploration repeats history in opening new worlds.

Not all the places they visited were equally exotic. Indeed, some became delightfully homelike. Honolulu was the center of whaling in the Pacific, and by the time Eliza Williams and Mary Lawrence visited there it had become a miniature New England — with a few improvements. "It is beautiful and green with nice flowers and patches of Yarrow and Bananas growing," wrote Eliza Williams after her first visit. "It is a pretty place . . . and reminds me much of home. I went out shopping two or three times and thought it a good deal like shopping at home." Some wives stayed at boarding-houses for a few months while their husbands went back out to sea; relieved of any personal responsibility for housekeeping, they kept up a lively social life that would have been considered quite frivolous in staid New England. There were supper parties and band concerts and tea parties and croquet parties and picnics and horseback rides along the beach. When whalers anchored at Honolulu, the captains and their wives joined in the gay whirl of activity. "Saw many acquaintances while in port," wrote Mary Lawrence, "some being home friends and others acquaintances of the voyage, especially captains and their wives, of whom there were many in port. We would generally meet at some boarding place, five or six couple, and after spending an hour or two very pleasantly, would adjourn to an ice-cream saloon." Another whaling wife wrote of her stay in Honolulu, "I kept wondering if I had died and gone to heaven." Some were probably glad enough to get out to sea again to recover from all the excitement.

The time at sea was broken up by visiting — known by whalers as "gamming" — with other ships. Everyone was always particularly pleased to gam what was called a "lady ship," that is, a ship with one or more females aboard. A homesick captain who had no wife along was pleased at the chance to spend a day in a family atmosphere. Sailors who had seen no women for months appreciated the chance to look at one. And women who had lived for months in all-male company looked forward to a visit most of all. When a ship came into view, women would search the deck for the sight of a figure garbed in skirts, and if the weather was too rough to gam or the men were in a hurry to follow the whales, the women would vigorously wave their handkerchiefs to celebrate their meeting.

A flourish of handkerchiefs, however, was a disappointing substitute for a real gam. Gamming was strictly a whalers' ritual, developed in a seafaring enterprise where exchange of information was more important than getting to a destination. And a ritual it was, with an etiquette as elaborate as that of a ballroom dance. It began with the operation known as "speaking a ship." Merchant ships and naval vessels never used this device; they simply hoisted signal flags, which was faster — and also safer. In speaking a ship, the two vessels maneuvered in a set sequence that quickly brought them close enough so that the captains could speak to each other without the aid of a speaking trumpet. To a novice watching for the first time as the final shearing off by one ship allowed the other to slip by the stern, it seemed as though a collision had barely been avoided. The operation needed a steady hand at the wheel to avoid such an embarrassment, and when the wind was brisk and the steering particularly uncertain, two men might be put at the wheel with an officer close by to watch them. New hands had been known to become so frightened the first time at the wheel while speaking a ship that they froze up and were incapable of executing orders or even ran from their post. But the whaling captains knew what they were doing, and their ships were no more likely to collide than were dancers at a court minuet.

When the ships came together, the captains had a

conversation — about whales, and weather, and reefs, and other ships in the area, and letters or news from home. Usually the conversation ended with one captain inviting the other to gam. If one ship was a lady ship, it received the visitor because a lady ship was always more homelike and the transfer from one ship to another was a delicate operation, a challenge for the men, and even more difficult for women encumbered by long skirts and petticoats. It was not only the captains who visited. During a gam half of each crew joined half of the other so they could do some gossiping of their own; and when the captains gathered on one ship, the mates went aboard the other. The whaleboats were used to carry people across; because all the regular places were filled, it was the custom for the captain to stand without holding onto anything, preferably keeping his hands in his pockets to show how good his sea legs were. It was an impressive display when it worked, but a sudden pitch of the boat could tumble the captain into the sea. If both ships had ladies aboard or there was some other reason for a woman to cross to another ship, she had some strong arms to help her into the boat and a convenience known as a "gamming chair" to help her up the side. This might be a regular armchair or a redesigned barrel rigged with a seat and a rope sling in which the lady in her visiting clothes could be hoisted down into and up out of the boat. This was a necessity when the water was rough, but when it was calm and men to haul the rope were needed for other work, women managed to go up and down the rope ladders even with their cumbersome skirts. In the last years of the century, one whaling wife began to wear bloomers at sea. But by that time the fashion was accepted on shore for such sports as bicycling. In the heyday of whaling a woman in bloomers was considered a radical feminist, and whaling wives were certainly not that.

The visit itself, especially when two or more ladies were involved, became a typical Victorian social call. Sometimes a dozen or more ships hunting whales in the same region would all come together and there would be an orgy of gamming, much as if the ladies were passing to each other's houses on a street in Nantucket or New Bedford. Captains and ladies exchanged gifts — preserves and cookies, pets of all sorts, from kittens to crickets, flowers in pots, and curiosities of various kinds. There was also some useful trading. Mary Lawrence, enjoying several days of gamming in the Bering Sea in June 1858, was able to record with satisfaction that "Mrs. Skinner and myself made an exchange of articles that we most wanted. I wanted a skein of red sewing silk very much (I had plenty that was too light), which she could supply me with, while she wanted a skein of blue yarn, which I had for her." Visits might even continue overnight. By putting three in a bunk, the captain on the sofa, and sometimes some bedding on the cabin floor, visits could be prolonged indefinitely. No woman who had been starved for feminine companionship ever complained about the crowding. One day in August 1853, Susan Folger Fisher of the *Cowper* came back from gamming with the captain's wife on the *Rod-man* to find four ladies from other ships waiting for her. All of them were old friends and they stayed the night, getting their fill of each other's company while they could. "It really seemed delightful," Susan Fisher wrote in her journal, "to have someone to talk with, besides getting whales." But getting whales was the reason for being at sea, and gams were possible only when they did not get in the way of business. "In a few hours we shall be many miles apart," Susan Fisher added, "so farewell female society for the present."

As the whaling ships went their separate ways, the people aboard each were closed into their isolated world once again. Time could drag for everyone, especially when no whales were sighted for days or weeks. To help time pass, American whalers developed the unique craft known as scrimshaw, which involves carving or engraving designs on whale teeth or bone. Men far from home took pleasure in making gifts for loved ones: pie crimpers and rolling pins for mothers whose pastry they would not taste again until the voyage was done, embroidery bodkins and spool holders for the little wife who always looked so charming bent over her fancy work, and — most popular — an elaborately decorated busk, the stiff piece for the front of a corset, for all the females left behind whose tightly laced shapes were so appealing. Along with designs of hearts, flowers, and lovebirds and of ships, sailors, and whales, literate sailors might add a few words: "Remember Me When Fare

Away," or something similar. One sailor engraved a verse on the busk he intended to present to his sweetheart:

> Accept, dear Girl this busk from me;
> Carved by my humble hand.
> I took it from a Sparm Whale's Jaw
> One thousand miles from land!
> In many a gale, has been the Whale,
> In which this bone did rest,
> His time is past, his bone at last
> Must now support thy brest.

The whaling captain whose family was along did not have to delay the pleasure of gift giving and passed his idle hours making presents for birthdays or Christmas, knowing he would be there to see his family enjoy them.

Scrimshaw was an art learned in the forecastle, where the crew berthed. That was where the captain had learned it. His wife would usually turn to more familiar occupations when time lay heavy on her hands. Some women enjoyed music. A surprising number managed to bring along a piano, melodeon, or parlor organ, which was often sold to a missionary on some remote Pacific island for a good profit when the whaler began its homeward passage. One woman managed to organize a sort of orchestra among the mates and had them play for her after supper. The fourth mate of the *Gazelle* recorded in his journal: "Two violins, tambourine, and a coal chisel. Made more noise than music, I guess, but answers for pastime." There were never many books on a

whaler, but reading the Bible absorbed the time of reli-
gious-minded women, especially on Sundays. Finally,
there was the journal, the same kind of book so useful
to women everywhere in America in the nineteenth century, into which they could pour their fears and joys
and observations on the world around them.

The first whaling wife to keep a journal was the first
whaling wife to go to sea — Mary Russell. She did not
keep one on her first voyage, but did on the second when
her son William was a fully qualified member of the
crew. She automatically grabbed her journal when she
felt helpless or did not know what else to do. One entry
she wrote during a gale records that William had just
come into the cabin to "comfort" her with the information that the ship might be about to sink. Then he
returned to work, leaving her to scribble her prayers in
the book. Eliza Williams also used her journal to comfort herself when conditions were upsetting. One morning, the *Florida* took a whale — certainly nothing for
the captain's wife to complain about; but Eliza Williams
was just a bit troubled by watching the killing: "I went
on deck a little while the boats were fast to him. I stood
looking over the stern at him, the poor fellow was too
much exhausted to run but was laying still the most of
the time, rolling and spouting thick blood. I was aston-
ished on looking through the glass at him to see how
thick he threw the blood out of his spout holes. They
were quite near to the ship and I could see plain all the
movements of the boats. The whale went down and
stopped some minutes and when he came up it seemed

as if he threw the blood thicker than before. He came up near the boats and threw blood all in the boats and all over some of the men. I did not like to look at the poor whale in his misery any longer and so came down below to write a few words about it." Presumably writing a description of the gory scene made it easier to handle.

Mary Lawrence celebrated her tenth wedding anniversary at sea by composing a three-stanza poem in her journal, concluding:

> Stoics have smiled and poets talked
> Of love's first fitful boons;
> But we in heightening bliss have walked
> 'Neath scores of "honey moons."

Her husband spent the day watching for whales.

The children who went whaling had toys and games to play with and lessons to learn, but some imitated their mothers and fathers by keeping a daily record. Laura Jernegan began hers on Sunday, December 1, 1868, when she was six years old: "It is Sunday and a very pleasant day. I have read two story books. This is my journal. Good Bye For To Day." Dated entries give a child's perspective on the important events of three years at sea. "They have taken four sperm whales. It is nice fun to see them," she wrote in December. "There is a fly on my finger. He has flew of now," she observed in January. In February 1871 she made more sophisticated entries: "We have 135 barrels of oil, 60 of humpback and 75 of sperm," was her comment on the family business. As for other forms of wildlife: "We had too birds, there is one now. One died. There names were Dick and Lulu. Dick died. Lulu is going to." And sure enough, the next entry begins "Lulu died last night." Sometimes, however, Laura clearly failed to find relief from boredom in journal writing. She started out one entry commenting on the work going on: "the men are boiling out the blubber in the try pots. the pots are real large. when the men are going to boil out the blubber, too men get in the pots and squis out the blubber and are way up to there knees of oil. when the men at the mast head say there she blows, Papa gives them 50 pounds of tobacco." After this effort the girl must have thought her own activity all the more boring by contrast. "I can't think of much to write," she went on. "I went to bed last night and got up this morning. we had baked potatoes for supeper, and biscute. would you like to hear some news   well I dont know of any."

Even grown women, well accustomed to using the journal to keep themselves alert to the details of their surroundings and ward off feelings of monotony, occasionally found that the routine of a whaler offered precious little stimulation. "I want something new to write about," Eliza Williams complained after a year and a half aboard the *Florida*. "I have nothing now but the same thing over and over, unless I give a description of our hog stock, which I might do if I felt much interested, for it is not to be sneezed at. We have about 40 little pigs since we left Ascension, and nice ones, too." As journals properly managed often do, the act of writing down a desire suggested a solution. Eliza Williams eventually became considerably interested in the *Florida*'s live-stock. After another year and a half had passed, and the *Florida* was on her way home, Eliza Williams recorded in her journal, "We have butchered a nice pig today, quite fat and very nice leafs of lard; she weighed 200 lbs. It shows what can be done in the pork line on ship board; she was raised on board this ship and is of the Wellington Island breed."

Ultimately an interest in some sort of real work was essential to avoid being overwhelmed by the monotony of life at sea. The whaling itself was unfamiliar work to women coming on board for the first time, and they naturally tended to look for occupation in those areas that were woman's work at home. It is hardly surprising that the barnyard animals caught their attention. "As I went on deck," Mary Lawrence wrote, "the first sight that greeted my eyes was the pigs and chickens running about at large on deck. Altogether they made an appearance so homelike that I could hardly realize that I was thousands of miles away from home." Of course, the captain's wife had her social position to consider, and she did not become a servant aboard the ship her husband commanded. She could, however, take an interest: "It is not quite as pleasant on deck as it has been," Eliza Williams wrote after a walk, "for we have a great many hogs and ducks, also 5 large turtles up there running about, that we bought at the Wellington's Island. The Men try to keep them forward but they will get aft sometimes, and when they do they make the deck quite dirty, though the Officers soon have the Men clean it off nice."

As this quotation suggests, the homelike atmosphere provided by livestock could become excessive. The deck of the *Florida* was only 123 feet long, and just a little over 30 feet wide. Yet there were sometimes more than a hundred chickens running about, and, in addition to the pigs, ducks, and turtles, a goat and a kid. Mary Lawrence, who had a similar assortment of animals on board, was a bit overwhelmed by a sudden explosion of the pig population in the spring of 1858. The first litter of six was welcome when it arrived on March 23, and so was the second, the appearance of which was recorded on March 29: "Had another addition to our family today of six more little pigs. The others are running about the deck and are very cunning." On April 6 there was "an addition again to our family of five pigs, which is rather more than we care about at this time." When five more were born on April 11, they "were very short-lived, as we already had more than we could accomodate."

As with many other familiar activities, raising livestock at sea was a bit different than it was on land. On land excess piglets could be sold or traded. And on land one was not threatened by accidents such as that which befell Mrs. Bryant of the *America* who, Mary Lawrence heard, "was quite seriously injured by the hog house fetching way and pressing her up against the side of the ship while they were cutting in a whale." Also, more than at home, there was a temptation to make pets of the animals, who really seemed to be part of the family confined to the floating world of the ship. Mary Lawrence sadly recorded the last moments of a pet hen named Hannah Butler: "Saw a school of porpoises this afternoon. As the men were hurrying forward preparing to strike them, one of them frightened Hannah Butler, and she flew overboard. As soon as she touched the water, the birds (gonies and mallemucks) dove down in pursuit of her. I felt very sorry, for I have a sort of affection for everything that has life on board, and she had become quite tame."

In addition to barnyard animals, an extraordinary variety of other creatures became pets on whalers. Dogs and cats were supplemented by such things as Japanese crickets, seals, and in one case a kangaroo. Caroline Mayhew was so fond of the kangaroo she was given in New Zealand as a present by the Maoris, who had acquired it in Australia, that she kept it at sea with her for several voyages. This well-traveled animal eventually ended its life in Mrs. Mayhew's home on Martha's Vineyard, where it was greatly admired by the local children. Birds were popular pets, because their singing was one of the things those at sea missed most. Mary Lawrence tried repeatedly to keep shore birds alive in her cabin, but they all died, until finally one called Susie made the adjustment. When she took it on deck for the first time, far out in the Pacific, "the air resounded with a perfect gush of melody." Pigeons, parakeets, and other exotic birds also became ship pets. One wife had a gray eagle. It had swooped down one day in an attempt to capture the cabin boy's dog. Instead it was captured and tamed, staying with the ship and taking the main royal yard as its favorite perch. Eliza Williams admired a pair of canaries owned by a woman she gammed with, and a few months later was delighted to receive a pair of her own on another gam.

Pets could be a pleasure, but they might also lead to tears. Children, especially, were upset to find a pet pig or chicken, particularly one named for a friend or relative, on the dinner table. And on a whaler, slippery decks, high seas, and boiling blubber were threats to life for shore-based creatures. Parnell Fisher of the *Alaska* had a series of incidents to mourn. First her "poor little canary" died; "It was so much to me and to the Capt." Then she recorded, "My little bird is well but the hens keep dying off. Only 6 left. Our cockatoo ate copper and died. Our cat a skeleton or an apology for one. We had four pigs but one was drowned in hot fat so he was made to grace our table." And Lucy Smith, whose mood was never cheerful, cried when one of her canaries escaped from its cage and flew away.

Far better than canaries and piglets for keeping the captain's wife from suffering boredom at sea were children. Azubah Cash wrote of her infant son Murray, who had been with her and his father aboard the whaler *Columbia* since he was two months old, "He is a pet and I hope he will be spared to us, he takes up time that might be spent less profitably." A hint of what could happen to a woman without such occupation is given in the diary of the third mate of the *Gazelle*, whose name is un-

known but who was obviously a sullen young man who
had no sympathy for Jane Worth, the captain's wife.
The captain and the other mates clearly adored her,
partly, one suspects, because her illness, which was both
physical and mental, brought out their Victorian gal-
lantry. "The mate hangs about her from morning till
night a standing by to run and make molasses candy or
whittles out a flower or wrap a shawl over her or any of
the pretty things that is wished," sniffed the junior officer. "She can lead him off by the nose or in any way
she chooses. Little bedsteads are made to please her . . .
and all of the playthings that a girl of 6 or 10 years old
cares for. Second childhood has commenced at the age
of 31." Once he came upon Jane Worth when she did
not know she was being observed: "Looking into the
after cabin today I saw in a cradle two dolls and beside
them sat a pretended mother singing and talking to them
as a little girl would. It is useless to write any more
about that but I formed my opinion."

Children were not a cure for mental illness, but they
were no doubt helpful in preserving mental health among
whaling wives who felt they had no other useful occupation aboard aside from tending their offspring. And
they might well have more than one baby aboard —
Eliza Williams reported her conversation with Captain
Philips of the *Arctic*, who had brought four children as
well as his wife with him on his previous voyage. Mrs.
Philips probably felt one voyage like that was enough.
Eliza Williams went to sea without her two children,
but gave birth twice before returning home. Her son

was born during "the heaviest gale we have had since we left home," and two years and one month later, a daughter was born while the *Florida* was anchored in Banderas Bay on the coast of Mexico. Many wives, like Azubah Cash, stopped on shore when their children were due, but births at sea were not uncommon. The captains referred to the babies born during the whaling season as young "bowheads."

Child rearing aboard a whaler presented some special problems in addition to the standard ones always faced by mothers. Laura Jernegan's little brother Prescott became so accustomed to the constant movement of the ship that he was afraid of land. The first time he was taken to Honolulu he cried when told to get out of the boat. Some toddlers who would trot confidently across a rolling deck had to learn to walk all over again when they went ashore. But the roll and pitch of a ship, especially in heavy weather, meant greater risk of falls.

The first mother on a whaler, Mary Russell, recorded an accident of her younger son Charles on the *Emily*. The boy tripped in the cabin companionway, tumbled down the stairs, and broke his arm just above the wrist. Such accidents were particularly unpleasant when, as on shipboard, there was no doctor to attend to the case and no pain-killing drugs except alcohol and laudanum, which is an opium derivative. Neither seemed appropriate for a seven-year-old child with a relatively minor injury, so his father treated him as he would have an adult: a sailor held him down while the injured arm was cracked back in place and bound in a splint. "The dear fellow bore the operation with courage that would have done credit to a man," wrote his mother.

Azubah Cash treated the case herself when her four-teen-month-old son "fell off the transom head first and struck his collar bone near the right shoulder against the stovebox." She thought it might be broken, but "all I could do was to put a bandage under his arm and round his neck and bathe it in spirits."

Eliza Williams's son Willie fell off a chest and cut his lip so badly his father had to put a stitch in it. "The poor little Fellow bore it better than I thought he would," wrote his mother. But the next day, Willie somehow got the stitch loose and it had to be sewed up again. "He did not like to have it done very well," wrote his mother.

At least such accidents were not fatal. The great fear of a mother at sea was that a little one would fall over-board. Laura Jernegan always remembered her mother's terror one day when she and her brother were on deck and there was a loud splash. It had, fortunately, not been Prescott — just a rotten pumpkin of about his size that the cook had tossed over the side. Throwing things over the side became a great game for little Willie Wil-liams. His mother recorded a game with Captain Fish's family that included their young sons. "Willie enjoyed it much and was as mischievous as usual. He threw his Hat and Willie Fish's overboard and one Shoe, but we got them." Mary Lawrence had a sadder event to record with respect to her six-year-old daughter, Minnie: "Minnie met with about as severe affliction as she ever

Whalers 133

experienced today," she wrote. "She lost her Frankie overboard, a doll that she dearly loved for its own sake and the more because it was Grandma Annie's. She cried for a long time and wrung her hands in the greatest agony." Finally her mother decided to let her go into formal mourning for the departed Frankie. "She insisted so much upon having black clothes made to wear that I was obliged to get a piece of black ribbon to tie on her arm to pacify her." Perhaps Minnie was able to comfort herself with one of her other dolls — her mother had made her a new one called Mary Stuart a few months earlier.

Periods of monotony aboard whalers were broken by periods of intense activity whenever a whale was taken. Such times made increasing demands on the mother of a toddler. The day the *Nautilus* took its first whale, Lucy Smith recorded her perspective of events: "I was so afraid of an accident. I was on deck all day, for Freddie was so excited I could not keep him below nor trust him on deck unless I was with him, as everyone had enough to do without taking care of him. I have got my face badly sunburned." Eight months later Freddie had not become much more manageable when whales were sighted. "Freddie is very troublesome when the boats are all down," his mother wrote, "and I have no time to read or meditate. When all the boats are down there is only the steward, cooper, and a sick man left."

In particular, Lucy Smith felt the absence of the "captain's servants" — the cook and cabin boy who, with others, were commonly expected to assist with tending the captain's children. Indeed, cooks, cabin boys, and stewards often remained with the captain's family as domestic servants between voyages. The usual baby sitter on shipboard was the cabin boy, who, as soon as he was big enough, went in a boat when whales were hunted. In quieter times, these youngsters spent much of their time keeping an eye on the captain's children.

Helen Jernegan, Laura and Prescott's mother, found life on the *Roman* quite pleasant and comfortable, largely because she had good servants: "There were none of us sick, and in the pleasant weather we enjoyed being on deck and watching the sailors at work, and there was always the prospect of seeing whales. I used to teach Laura in the morning, and she learned very quickly; we had a small room built on deck, and she sat at a table to study her lessons. Prescott was happy all day in playing with ropes, and he also had a swing, and the small cabin boy used to amuse him. When they caught a whale and brought him side of the ship, there were lively times on board, as this made all the sailors happy, as they would have their share of the money. There were a great many nice stores put in the ship for the cabin and we had a good cook, so I did not miss home food, and we nearly always had fowl and eggs."

Good servants were even more important when there was sickness. Eliza Williams went to gam aboard the *South Boston,* where the captain's wife had been seasick steadily for five months. Mrs. Reynolds was glad to have a visitor, and told her guest it was the first time she had sat up all day for some time. She had a nine-month-old son with her. "He is the most pleasant, quiet Child, I think, I ever saw," wrote Eliza Williams, "and well for her it is, for she has not been able to take care of it. She has an excellent Cabin Boy. He does everything for the Child, washes, irons, and even sews for it. He washes and dresses it, feeds it, and puts it to sleep. I don't see what she would do without him."

As was the case with women of equivalent social class on shore, whaling captains' wives did only that work they chose to do. Indeed, it was considered as unsuitable for the captain's wife to enter the galley as it would be for the southern plantation mistress to invade the territory of her black kitchen staff. The cook and the steward prepared and served the meals to the captain's family and the officers in the cabin, usually in two shifts, with the senior officers taking turns eating with the captain's shift. The crew ate in the forward part of the ship. The menus were not the same, any more than they would have been for family and servants on shore. On Christmas Day, for instance, Mary Lawrence recorded, "We sat down to a Christmas dinner of two roast turkeys, sweet and Irish potatoes, boiled onions, stewed pumpkin, and cranberries, pickles, and a nice Indian pudding made of milk and eggs. Had a goat killed for the benefit of those living in the forecastle, to which, I should think, they did ample justice, as there are but two legs remaining." When Minnie celebrated her eighth birthday she was allowed to invite all of the officers to her birthday party. "The officers united in saying they

had not sat down to such a table since they left home.
The treat consisted of a plate of sister Celia's fruitcake,
two loaves of cupcake frosted, two plates of currant jelly
tarts, and a dish of preserved pineapple, also hot coffee,
good and strong, with plenty of milk and white sugar.
After we had finished, there was an ample supply left,
which was sent into the steerage for boatsteerers,
etc."

Not every captain would have been so generous in
distributing food to the forecastle. Costs of feeding the
crew came out of the profit to be made by the voyage.
The third mate of the *Gazelle*, obviously a hungry teenager, complained constantly about having poorer food
than the captain's table. "One kind of coffee has to be
made for the Capt. and wife and mate, another for the
three inferior officers, and another for the boatsteerers,
and cook makes one more kind of rye for the men."
Again, "I eat two meals of victuals today. Our dinner
consisted of raw duff and sour molasses." He and the
second mate "live nearly the same as the men in the
forecastle while they are gloating over green corn, sau-
sages, layer cake, doughnuts, potatoes, and onions."
When the owners — of whom the captain usually was
one — were determined to maximize profit, food in the
forecastle could be pretty awful: salt beef or pork three
times a day and the bread known as hard tack. All of
these staples could become much the worse for wear
after a year or two in casks. One man who served on a
whaler recalled the practice in the forecastle of dropping
hard tack into hot coffee to soak out the worms, which

could then be skimmed off the top of the coffee before drinking it. When such conditions were common, sailors did not resent the condescension involved when a captain's lady sent them leftover pastries and allowed them a treat of fresh goat meat on Christmas.

Meanwhile, in the aft section of the ship, women cooked as upper-class ladies did on shore, only in an emergency or for fun. Willie Williams remembered that his mother often made up a special dish for afternoon tea, and Mary Lawrence recorded one evening before an anticipated day of gamming, "After dinner I made some cake to put away, for as we are in the midst of ships, it is likely that we shall have more or less company while there is no whaling to do." She also recorded making pies, preserves, and an old-fashioned New England Indian pudding. Once, when Minnie had another little girl gamming on board, they were allowed to amuse themselves by cooking. "Today they made cake and cookies, which were really quite nice," Mary Lawrence wrote, "but I imagine they had a little of the steward's assistance."

The Lawrences seem to have enjoyed cooking; even the captain invaded the galley one day to make up a fish chowder. And when the steward and the steerage boy had other work to do, Mary Lawrence was not above pitching in to help the cook get dinner. But it was the cook's problem, not hers, when, one evening, "in shipping a sea, everything was taken from the stove by the roll of the ship, fish, potatoes, meat, and coppers all rolling around the deck together." Because of this acci-

dent, "our cook was obliged to get two suppers tonight," with the captain's wife commenting only, "Such
terrible times are not very common." We can also be
sure that it was the steward's problem, not Mary Lawrence's, when there was cleaning up to do after one of
her culinary undertakings: "As we were to have roast
pork for dinner, I thought I would have a luxury in the
shape of stewed apple for sauce, as we had a few apples
left. So I prepared them, sent and borrowed a saucepan of the cook, stewed them very nicely, sweetened
them, and was just preparing to take them up when there
came an extra roll which was a little more than I could
manage; and my applesauce was spattered all around on
the cabin floor, and the saucepan went into the pantry."

Washing and cleaning were other forms of women's
work that the captains' ladies did only when they wanted
to. Most preferred doing their own laundry, probably
because the servants on the ship could not meet their
standards with respect to starching and ironing their
lingerie and the family's good clothing. Lucy Smith arranged with the *Nautilus* cook to do her family's washing for an extra $1.50 a month, but soon afterward her
diary records that she was again doing it herself, waiting
impatiently for weather good enough to dry clothing on
deck. Sometimes the captain gave her a hand hanging
out the clothes or taking them down.

The weather was the main factor in choosing a washing day. Women might have to wait a month for a day
that was not wet or foggy. Mary Lawrence seized the
opportunity one sunny morning after she had gone four

weeks without a wash day. Then, "Just as I got about half through, the fog came thicker than I ever saw it before. I was obliged to put my white clothes in soak and dry the colored clothes in the cabin." Three days later she decided to try to dry the clothes on the deck, even though there was a strong breeze, hoping they would dry quickly. "So the consequence was that I have old rags enough now to supply the whole ship. I found how they were going and took them in the cabin to dry, not, however, until several garments were torn past mending."

Ironing was an even harder job than washing. "Have finished washing but my ironing will take some time," Lucy Smith wrote, "as I have ten bosom shirts, two starched dresses, besides several doz collars and cuffs." The next day, she "began ironing at eight A.M. and ironed until three this afternoon. My hands are almost blistered holding on to the iron," she added. "I feel very tired." Ironing was done with the same heavy instrument heated on a stove that was used by women on shore, but shipboard conditions again made a difference. Eliza Williams recorded an occasion when the weather was good for washing but impossible for ironing. "It has been a pleasant sunshiny day, but the wind blowing almost a gale and the Ship rolling very badly. I have been trying to iron a little, but cannot keep my iron on the stove, so have given it up for today."

Cleaning the family's quarters was another operation the captain's wife might take a hand in when she chose. "I need not do any of the cleaning, except that I do it

from choice, as then I know it is clean," wrote Mary
Lawrence. She "wiped up a little" every Saturday to
supplement the efforts of the steward and the cabin boy.
The other members of the family sometimes pitched in
too. "Samuel and myself cleaned our bedroom, while
Minnie took hers in her own hands and succeeded very
well, needing but very little help from me." The major
cleaning aboard a whaler, however, was an operation a
captain's wife had no part of.

Whaling was very dirty work; it was the work of a
slaughterhouse. The enormous carcass of a dead whale,
often longer than the ship, was butchered and the blubber boiled down for oil. Since much of the butchering
was done while the carcass was in the water, the operation was cleaner than it might have been, but the boiling
always made a mess. Furthermore, a dead whale — one
that was recovered from a beach or had escaped with a
harpoon in it and was dead when brought to the ship —
smelled abominably. The sailors spoke of a dead whale
as a "stinker"; another ship that had taken one had no
need to announce the fact. "Spoke the *Good Return* in
the forenoon," wrote Mary Lawrence, "cutting in a dead
whale which she picked up in the morning. Our olfac-
tory nerves assured us that it was so some time before
we spoke him." Having such an object decomposing
alongside one's own ship and then boiling in the try
works was even worse. But for whaling wives, it was the
smell of money. "I can bear it all first rate," wrote Eliza
Williams, "when I consider that it is filling our ship all

the time and by and by it will all be over and we will go home."

The better the whaling at the moment, the filthier the ship. The *Nautilus* crew had recovered a stinker and killed a whale of its own when Lucy Smith observed, "Our vessel is the dirtiest place I ever saw as there has been no chance to clean up as there is the blubber of one whale on deck besides casks of oil and the oil has run out of the blubber so it is frequently scooped up off the deck. They have now nearly finished trying the stinking blubber and got the blubber room nearly cleared. The blubber on deck will not smell so."

For all the social barriers between the captain's quarters and the forecastle, a whaler was a small place and when boiling was done nothing stayed clean. "I have done no work for two days past except a little mending," wrote Lucy Smith. "The ship is so dirty that I do not like to get out any work. Freddie is in the midst of everything, as dirty as a little pig, then, rubbing around me, together with what I get from the ship, my clothes are too dirty to take any work on."

Willie Williams was at least as bad as Freddie Smith. On a day when the *Florida* was boiling blubber and calking decks, Eliza Williams wrote, "Willie has a good time with it all, and between the Oil and Tar, I can't keep him clean an hour." But it was no easier to keep the filth off her infant daughter. "We are a dirty looking people altogether," wrote Eliza Williams, "not excepting the baby, the dirt has got all over the ship." Of course some people got dirtier than others. Eliza Williams noted, "The Men are just as greasy and smutty as they can be, not excepting the Captain, who manages to get into all the dirty work he can." Washing these work clothes and cleaning the deck after a boiling operation was a far more challenging undertaking than laundering the baby's dresses and mopping up the captain's quarters.

On a well-run ship, the crew that had been working day and night boiling out the blubber would get only a short break for rest and food before being put to work cleaning up. Merchant seamen, who had passed a whaler boiling out a stinker, spread the idea that both whalers and their ships were the foulest things afloat — even worse than slavers. But whaling captains knew as well as any others that dirt was bad for discipline. When little Willie Williams grew up and became a member of his father's crew, he learned that "every good first mate had an obsession for cleanliness; it helped to keep the crew busy and a busy crew had little time or inclination for plotting mischief." Some, indeed, grumbled about the orders that kept them scrubbing to meet a demanding captain's standards. It was said that the captain of the *Charles W. Morgan* did not feel cleaning was done until "you would have found it hard work to soil a white pocket handkerchief by rubbing it on any part."

The scum of fat that covered everything from the blubber room to the yardarms was scoured away with saltwater mixed with lye from the try works ashes, a combination, according to Willie Williams, "that will remove anything known as dirt, including the skin on your hands." The clothing was soaked in a mixture of saltwater and urine, which had enough grease-cutting ammonia to loosen the worst of the soil. It was then scrubbed in saltwater in a tub with a pounding barrel. A captain's wife would, of course, have nothing to do with the crew's clothing, but Mary Lawrence, at least, "assisted" her husband with his washing when the temperature in the wash house on deck was not too cool for her.

How did women like Mary Lawrence and Eliza Williams perceive their role at sea? At first glance one might think they would have felt isolated and alienated from the major activities around them. Could a lone woman living for years with thirty or forty men, most of them so far beneath her socially that it was scarcely decent for her to speak to them, feel anything but an intruder? Or did these women, perhaps, see themselves as opening new doors for their sex by proving they could endure the hardships of the most arduous seafaring life as well as males? Surprisingly, role conflict appears to have troubled whaling wives not at all. They were conventional Victorian women who transferred their perception of themselves as homemakers virtually unchanged from land to sea.

For the Victorians, homemaking did not mean doing domestic chores so much as maintaining an emotional environment of peace and moral uplift. Men, it was believed, required the presence of a "mother" to keep them well behaved and civilized. Thus, simply by being aboard the ship, a woman could feel she was conferring important benefits on the extended "family" in the forecastle as well as in the cabin. Missionaries active in the Pacific were particularly emphatic in extolling the value of females to the whaling industry. "A few years ago it was exceedingly rare for a Whaling Captain to be accompanied by his wife and children, but it is now very common," wrote the Reverend Samuel C. Damon in 1858. "The happy influence of this goodly number of ladies is apparent to the most careless observer."

Many whaling wives were deeply religious, but even those who carried their piety more lightly took seriously the role of "angel of the house," as Victorian literature often expressed it. Mary Brewster, the first woman to go aboard a whaler into the Arctic Ocean, explained her reasons for making the voyage in her journal entry of May 2, 1849: "I am going and in the end hope I may be a useful companion, a soother of woes, a calmer of troubles and a friend in need . . . I pray kind Heaven to shine upon us to prosper and keep us from all danger and suffer no ill to betide all on board of this ship."

Praying for the crew was a duty of the captain's wife even if she could not speak to them, for the Victorians expected women to attend to such matters. Lucy Smith was distressed when a Pacific native known as "George Kanaka," who was a boatsteerer of the *Nautilus*, died and was buried at sea without having been properly Christianized. "I have never had any religious conversation with him," she wrote in her journal. "Oh how much I regret it. Had I thought he was so near eternity

I would have found an opportunity to speak to him of Jesus, but being the only female on board I have feared that if I should try to see and talk with him there would be some who scoff at religion that would talk about me and say I ought not to go into the steerage. I have wanted to do right and if I have sinned by neglecting my duty may God in mercy forgive me."

Mary Lawrence believed that what might be impropriety in herself could be done by her little daughter. And so Minnie brought religion to the forecastle. One Sunday her mother encouraged the girl to fill her doll carriage with Bibles and wheel it down to the crew's berthing area. "She came back very quick with an empty carriage, had it reloaded, and went again until she gave away every one that we had," wrote Mary Lawrence approvingly. "She said they all wanted one, even the Portuguese, that could read. I could but think they were taken far more readily from her than they would have been from anyone else. It may be we can do some good through her."

Before the voyage was done Minnie was running a Sunday school class. Listening to the sermons of the serious seven-year-old was no doubt a treat for the rough men, for, as her mother put it, she had "a great many strange and original thoughts." She had "a very strong desire to go to Asia. She wishes to see where the ark was, also to visit Shiloh and see the Tabernacle, to go to Jerusalem and see if she could not obtain a piece of the Cross; and today while she was conversing on the subject, she seemed to think that if she ever went, she should take a shovel with her and see if she could not find where Moses was buried on the mountain. She thinks that as he was such a good man that his body would not turn to clay as they do now."

Aboard the *Florida*, Eliza Williams presided over Sunday observances that she was pleased to find much more orderly and quiet than she expected with so many men. Her husband saw that "all work is laid aside Saturday night and nothing done on Sunday but what is necessary." On a warm, sunny New Year's Day, which was a Sunday, she wrote a prayer into her journal: "Oh, may we all aboard of this Ship be enabled to keep God ever before our eyes this year in all we do and say, and live as becometh Christian People, though we can't enjoy the privileges of religion as the People do at home." And she was well enough satisfied with the scene surrounding her that Sabbath: "The Men are all reading about the deck excepting those on duty. The Cabin Boys have been learning their lessons from the primer and reciting it to me. It really appears to me that the hogs, hens and ducks do not make as much noise as usual — the reason, I suppose, that they do not get driven about as much as on a week day."

Eliza Williams was perhaps as perfect an example of the ideal Victorian lady as could have been found anywhere in America, and it is easy to see why she was welcome at sea. Whaling wives came from a tradition that encouraged women to be strong and self-reliant. Because of the high death rate among seafaring men and the length of whaling voyages, whaling communities in

New England were overwhelmingly female. At one point women in Nantucket outnumbered the men four to one. In such communities, women were denied political rights — as they were everywhere in the nineteenth century — but, of necessity, they dominated all other activity in the town. Typically, a captain's wife kept the books for the family business and made arrangements to market the goods he brought home from a voyage, be they exotic commodities from China or casks of whale oil and bone. In addition, all local businesses were run by women — the groceries, bakeries, dry-goods stores, and so on. Indeed, in Newport, the main street in town, Centre Street, was popularly known as "Petticoat Row" because every single shop was managed by a woman.

A woman with feminist leanings might thrive in such an atmosphere. Eliza Williams did not like it at all. She did not like managing money matters while her husband was away. She felt uncomfortable collecting debts and deciding on new investments. She hated having to collect rent from her husband's brother-in-law, who was a sharecropper on her husband's farm. She was exactly the sort of shy, blushing, dependent female that the Victorians adored.

Furthermore, she looked the part. Eliza Williams was a tiny woman, even by the standards of the time. She weighed less than one hundred pounds; when her husband stood with his arm outstretched, she could stand beneath it without touching. Her photographs show a clear, unlined face, fine high cheekbones, light wavy hair, and enormous luminous eyes.

Her journal reveals what the Victorians would have called a "true woman's heart," cheerful, almost child-like in her pleasure at seeing new things, and overflowing with sympathetic feelings for those around her. All the routine work of whaling seemed to her so hard and dangerous; the crew of the *Florida*, accustomed to having such things taken for granted by the captain and their fellow sailors, thoroughly enjoyed the dainty lady's concern for their well-being and her admiration of their skills. She thought it was terrible that they had to work when the weather was wet and cold and go up in the rigging when the wind was blowing hard. She worried about them when they went out in their little boats, "though they laugh at my timidity," she wrote. "It was quite an exciting scene to me," she recorded in her journal after she had watched the *Florida*'s boats out hunting, "and mixed with a good deal of fear for the safety of those Men. It seemed to me that they were under the boats and every plunge would dash them in pieces. The Men on the Ship seem to enjoy the fun, for they would shout and laugh." Then, when they got a whale, they had to cut it all up. When it was done, Eliza Williams "was glad for the Men, for it seemed to me that they must be very tired, and such a bad place for them to work. It made me tremble to see them stand there on that narrow staging with a rope passed around their bodies and made fast to the Ship to keep them from going over, while they leaned forward to cut . . . The sharks were around the Ship and I saw one fellow, more bold than the rest, I suppose, venture almost to the whale to get a bite." She was even more frightened when "one of the stagings gave way and pitched the first Mate into the water." It surprised her that "he did not seem to mind that, for he was up and to work again, wet as he was; in fact they were all as wet as they could well be."

The captain's lady was such an appreciative spectator that the first mate decided to give her a real treat: "In the afternoon the Mate came to me and wanted me to go with him and take a look in the reception room, as he termed it. I went, and I could not refrain from laughter, at such a comical sight! There the Men were at work up to their waists in blubber. The warm weather had tried out the oil a good deal and made it soft. I don't see how they could stand in among it, but they were laughing and having a good deal of fun."

A woman's sympathetic heart could provide practical benefits for the sailors. Discipline aboard whalers, as aboard all nineteenth-century ships, was severe. Men might be put in irons, flogged, or beaten with a belaying pin on the authority of the captain. Usually the captain's wife went below while discipline was being enforced, confining herself to noting in her journal her distress at the need for punishment and her hopes that it would do the malefactor some good and cause him to reform. Sometimes, however, particularly with a captain who was known to be hot tempered, a wife would interfere. George Fred Tilton, a sailor who had been on a voyage with Lucy Smith aboard the *Abraham Barker*, recalled that she had interceded for him when the captain was about to put him in irons. Captain Smith does not seem to have been unusually severe, and Lucy Smith ordinarily accepted the need to punish members of the crew occasionally. But for some reason she felt the captain was wrong about George Fred Tilton. Tilton could not hear exactly what Lucy Smith said to her husband, but it made the captain angry. "Go below, Lucy," he had shouted at her. "Mutiny on my ship!" The old sailor recalled that "she didn't go though, and I didn't have any irons put on me, but I have always felt that if it hadn't been for her I would have been ironed and like enough worse things would have happened to me."

Captain John Norton was such a tyrant at sea that the restraining influence of his wife Charity was considered essential to the success of his voyages. An old sailor recalled, "There were some hard tickets among the whaling captains in those days, and he was one of the hardest of the lot. She had to go with him on his voyages. The owners used to beg her to go, because they knew it was their only chance." Without her, it was believed, the crew would murder their captain. Indeed, a sailor once told Captain Norton's nephew, who was also aboard, "I'd as soon kill the captain as I would a kitten, but I s'pose the old lady would feel bad." No one wanted to hurt "the old lady." A description has been preserved of Charity Norton in action during a voyage aboard the *Ionia* in 1868. Twelve men had tried to desert, and the captain recaptured them and had them tied up in the rigging. He intended to convince them of the benefits of staying with their ship by giving each a flogging with a rope whip. His wife came on deck after the first had been punished.

"John," she said to her husband, "what are those men in the rigging for?"

"I'm going to lick 'em," he said.

"Oh no you're not," said Charity Norton, and that was the end of it.

As their occasional defiance of their husbands in the crucial area of discipline suggests, the demure Victorian ladies who went whaling were tougher than they seemed on the surface. The same was true of those who went to live in pioneer homes on the western frontier or who kept southern plantations functioning during the Civil War. The air of weakness and helplessness that Victorians believed made a woman attractive was, after all, a set of deliberately cultivated mannerisms. It should be no more surprising to find that Victorian ladies could be strong and courageous than to find that a man who cultivates macho mannerisms is a coward and a weakling.

Even Eliza Williams was full of surprises when she had to confront a real emergency. Her son remembered two incidents in particular. The first occurred when one of the Pacific natives who had recently joined the crew went violently mad. He suddenly attacked a shipmate with a knife, and as the other men tried to corner and subdue the lunatic, Eliza Williams tended the wounded man. The sailor had been slashed across the abdomen; Willie Williams, who had helped him to a place in the shade by the cabin, saw that "his bowels were in his shirt." Nothing could be done for him except to give him water and bathe his forehead, which Eliza Williams did as the men around her shouted and pursued the madman with harpoons and a revolver and finally killed him with a rifle bullet. "I often marveled at my mother's courage and control of her nerves under real danger or trying conditions," Willie Williams wrote, "because in small matters she was timid and dreaded the sight of blood . . . Here was an awful situation; we were confined on a small craft in mid-ocean with a crazy man, but she was as cool as any man on the ship."

Williams also remembered his mother's coolness when the first mate was badly injured. While he was pursuing a whale, his bomb gun went off accidentally and the lance cut into his face from his lower jaw to a point above the eyebrow. It was a serious injury, but he did not lose consciousness, and as there were no anesthetics aboard, he had to be held down while the wound was stitched up. It took some time, and one officer after another had to be relieved from holding the patient's head steady. They were sickened by the blood and the agony the operation was causing their shipmate. Finally Eliza Williams took over and finished the job. "There was one feature of this incident which I cannot overlook," her son wrote later, "and that was the nerve and grit of one little woman compared to the big strong men." Indeed, he was willing to generalize from what he had seen of his mother in her whaling days. "In my experience," he wrote, "a woman can be depended upon to show true nerve and grit at the crucial moment better than a man."

It was not just at crucial moments that whaling wives revealed strength and ability beyond that necessary to maintain a homelike atmosphere for men at sea. Although when they first went with the ship, they were totally ignorant of the work involved in whaling, they did not remain ignorant for long. And as they learned something of the business, they found ways to be useful. As Susan Folger Fisher wrote from the *Cowper* in 1853 as boiling was going on, "Everyone on board is busy enough except myself and I have looked on until I am tired. I am not used to seeing so much business carried on without being able to lend a helping hand." Domestic chores were just not enough for women who, as the months passed, became ever more conscious of the connection between filling the oil barrels and going home. Gradually they concentrated increasingly on doing what they could to get those barrels filled.

Feminine skills often proved to have maritime application. Sewing, for example. Kate Mellen, who sailed with her husband aboard the *Europa*, demonstrated her value to her husband with her needle. "It is very convenient to have a woman aboard of your ship occasionally if for nothing more than to mend your stockings, sew on buttons, etc. etc.," he wrote. But sewing could go beyond clothing repair. Lucy Smith, who had a sewing machine aboard, used it to make a mainsail for one boat, a jib for another, and a canvas cover for the chronometer box. Mary Lawrence adopted the American flag as her special concern and spent many hours mending it. Perhaps it did not attract whales, but working on the

flag was working for the ship in a way that lengthening
Minnie's frocks and making her doll clothing was not;
and it probably was as useful in helping the *Addison*'s
hunts as her practice of taking off her shoes and throwing them after a boat crew lowering for a whale, a ritual
she superstitiously believed might bring them luck.

Women who kept their minds on the whales could
help in other ways too. The wife of Captain Charles A.
Grant spent thirty-two years at sea and had the distinction of winning one of the silver dollars her husband
always awarded the lookout who was the first to spot a
whale. She was hanging out her wash one day when she
saw the spouting of a big one and was the first person
to bellow, "There blows! blows! blows!" that got the
men running to lower the boats. Even more direct
wifely assistance was offered by the woman whose husband was a bit absent-minded. She ran after him once,
as he was lowering his boat, crying, "John, John, don't
forget your bomb-gun!"

No evidence has been found to indicate that any
whaling wife ever developed an ambition to go out in a
boat with a harpoon herself or to share in the dirty,
sweaty work of boiling out blubber. Nevertheless, a
small number of women whalers went in the boats,
sweated in the blubber rooms, and did all the work of
the regular crew. These women were not captains' wives,
but sailors who joined the crew after disguising their
sex. So long as the disguise was effective, they lived in
the forecastle, accepted as men.

There were certainly far fewer women sailors aboard

whalers than on warships or merchant vessels. Although
it is impossible to discover the motives of women who
went to sea in disguise — especially of those whose true
sex was never made public — some motives clearly
would not apply to whalers as they would to other ships.
Anyone needing free passage somewhere — to follow a
lover, escape from family pressures, or simply find adventure — would not choose a whaler. Whalers were not
headed anywhere, they went nowhere fast, and there was
nothing to do aboard them but hunt whales and make
scrimshaw. Of course some people simply enjoyed the
life, and some women enjoyed it enough to sacrifice a
normal sex life exactly as male sailors who went to sea
without women had to do. The first woman known to
have gone to sea on a whaler as a crew member signed
on aboard the ship *Lydia* before the end of the eighteenth century. When the ship returned to Nantucket
from a successful whaling voyage off the coast of Brazil,
the captain reported, as a matter of special interest, his
discovery that one of his crew, who had sailed two voyages undetected, was a female. Her name was not recorded.

The most common motive for women to go aboard
warships in disguise was to follow a man. At least one
woman went aboard a whaler for that reason. She had
met a young man in her home town in upstate New
York and fallen in love with him. When he had tired of
their relationship, he went off to Nantucket to sign on
for a whaling cruise. Not to be cast off so easily, she
followed him, and when she learned that a man answer-

ing her lover's description had signed on the *Mitchell*, she put on male clothing and signed on too. By the time she discovered that he was not aboard, the ship had cleared the harbor and it was too late. So she made the best of it. She knew nothing about whaling or sailing, of course, but neither did about half the crew. So-called greenhands normally made up a good part of the man-power on every whaler. They learned quickly enough if they wanted to stay alive, and the female "greenie" was soon climbing the rigging, pulling an oar in the whale boat, and cutting into the slippery back of a whale to slice off the blubber. When the *Mitchell* rounded the Horn at the tip of South America and was caught in a snow squall, she made a reputation for herself by being the only hand willing to climb out to cast off the hal-yards to loose the foretopsail and main while all the rest were hanging on to the weather rigging for dear life and would not go no matter how much the captain yelled and threatened.

Although she was popular with the officers, she never became one of the boys in the forecastle, largely because she did not swear or tell lewd stories. But no one sus-pected that she was not a male until she developed a fever while they were off the coast of Peru. As she lay delirious in her bunk in the tropical heat, she pulled open both her shirt and the tight corset cover she had worn since leaving port eight months earlier. The other men around her were asleep, but one of the hands on watch came below to fetch his pipe. He took one look, ran to tell the mate, and within minutes every man aboard had had a look and confirmed the fact that there was indeed a woman among them. The captain put straight into port and dropped her off at Lima.

Women who went aboard whalers deliberately generally planned better than the woman on the *Mitchell,* so they could keep their jobs even if, for some reason, they did reveal their sex. A woman known only by her male name, George Weldon, went whaling aboard the *America.* George Weldon fit right in with the others in the forecastle — swore, told dirty stories, got into fights, and drank and gambled whenever there was an opportunity. Weldon did a full share of the work too, but not so much as to win any praise from the officers. Indeed, some bad feeling developed between Weldon and the third mate. Their quarrel reached a crisis one day when Weldon was rowing in the third mate's boat, pursuing a whale with an iron already in it, and Weldon missed a stroke. The mate swore, and instead of accepting the tongue lashing, Weldon drew a knife and started for him. That was mutiny, the gravest of all crimes at sea, and when the boat returned to the ship and the incident was reported to the captain, he decided that a flogging was in order. That was when George Weldon asked to speak with the captain in private. There was no flogging on the *America;* the sailor accused of mutiny was sent back to work as though nothing had happened. The captain noted in his log, "This day I found George Weldon to be a woman."

Although whaling wives carefully observed the accepted role barriers for their sex and would have been horrified to find a disguised female in the forecastle, they often qualified themselves in nautical affairs to such an extent that they became ships' officers of a sort. A few regularly took a turn at the helm and stood watches. On the title page of her journal, Mary Lawrence proudly inscribed herself as "The Captain's *best* mate." Women who flaunted their authority a bit too openly might cause their husbands' ships to be referred to derisively as "hen frigates." Mark Twain drew a mocking portrait of a whaling wife he encountered in Honolulu, whose language reflected a greater grasp of her husband's business than he thought altogether seemly. "I have just met an estimable lady, Mrs. Captain Jollopson," he wrote, "whose husband (with her assistance) commands the whaling bark *Lucretia Wilkerson* — and she said: 'While I was laying off and on before the post office, here comes a shipkeeper around the corner three sheets in the wind and his deadlights stove in, and I see by the way he was bulling that if he didn't sheer off and shorten sail he'd foul my larboard stuns'l-boom. I backed off fast as I could, and swung out to him to port his helm, but it warn't no use; he'd everything drawing and I had considerable sternway, and he just struck me a little abaft the beam, and down I went, head on, and skunned my elbow. I shouldn't wonder if I'd have to be hove down.' "

The skill most commonly cultivated by whalers' wives, to enable them to participate more fully in the ship's business, was navigation. Indeed, Honor Earle was officially rated as navigator aboard the *Charles W. Morgan* when she sailed with her husband between 1890 and 1906. A former schoolteacher, she had no trouble mastering the mathematics needed to determine latitude and longitude; and she was glad to have something constructive to do at sea. "A whaler, you know, is not the place to have the liveliest time in the world," she explained, "so I applied myself to learning navigation."

Lucy Smith's husband taught her to take the position of the sun and make the calculations. After a few lessons she recorded with satisfaction, "I have taken the sun twice today, made the Lat. the same as George and Longitude within two miles and George says that is as near alike as two persons usually get the altitudes." The next day, her husband's calculations and hers were identical to the second.

On the *Florence*, no one but Captain Williams knew how to navigate when the ship put out to sea. Eliza Williams seems not to have learned, and none of the officers had any desire to learn either; indeed three of the four officers could not even read. But Willie learned to navigate, and even his little sister got some training in dead reckoning. Mary Williams frequently held the sand glass when the speed of the ship was being measured because, her brother said, it was "one thing a girl could do as well as a boy." By the time she was eight, Laura Jernegan was taking enough interest in navigation to record the ship's position in her journal from time to time.

No evidence has been found of any woman going to sea as captain of a whaler, but as Herman Melville observed, "In time of peril, like the needle to the lode-

stone, obedience, irrespective of rank, generally flies to
him who is best fitted to command." On a ship in the
middle of the ocean the "him" who was best fitted might
well be the captain's wife. Such was the case aboard the
Powhatan in 1846. Caroline Mayhew was a doctor's
daughter and had a practical knowledge of medicine;
she also knew the elements of navigation. When a small-
pox epidemic broke out aboard the *Powhatan* and Captain William Mayhew contracted the disease and was
unable to perform his duties, Caroline Mayhew did what
was necessary. She was the chief medical officer, navigator, and de facto captain until her husband recovered.
There was no resentment by the men. On the contrary,
they gave her full credit for having saved their lives.
When the crisis was past the sailors overwhelmed her
with gifts, the only things they had: scrimshawed pie-
jagging wheels, knitting needles inlaid with decorative
woods, and a swift, an elaborate device for winding yarn,
which was presented to her in an ivory box decorated
with her initials.

Life on a whaler was not for everyone. Some women
left their ships after a few months and took passage back
home or had to be left off in Hawaii or some other port
because seasickness or boredom at sea was more than
they could tolerate. Some stuck out the voyages but
hated every minute. Parnell Fisher could hardly wait for
her voyage aboard the *Alaska* to end. "Lowered for
whales, but got none," she wrote in her journal when
the oil casks were almost all filled, "Do hope we get one
more as Capt. has promised me if he gets one more he

will go home. I am so tired of the sea & not well but I do not wish to complain." Once back in Martha's Vineyard, Captain Fisher tried to make it up to his wife by building her a fine new house before he went off to sea again. She liked the old house better, though: she could not see the ocean from it.

Other women, however, throve on the whaling life. Their squat little ships that stank abominably when a dead whale was being boiled were viewed with horror not only by ladies who remained ashore but by other seafaring women as well. By the end of the whaling period, wives of clipper-ship captains had far more comfortable accommodations than any whaling wife. When Mary Lawrence visited the merchant vessel *John Gilpin* and saw the quarters of the captain's wife, she "wished very much for a small piece of her spacious cabin to enlarge mine a little." And when the *Addison* passed near a large steamship carrying passengers to California, Mary Lawrence admitted it was a "grand sight." She waved her handkerchief at the crowd of ladies on the deck. "I imagine that I was looked upon by them as an object of pity," she wrote in her journal later that day. "But I do not believe that I would exchange situations with any one of them." Those were the words of a true whaling wife!

5

Traders

WHALING WIVES certainly had no reason to complain about their living conditions if they compared their lot with that of most other nineteenth-century women. They were undoubtedly better off than the women crowded with their families into urban slums or struggling through the first difficult years on an isolated prairie farm. Yet whaling wives never saw the women who were working in sweatshops in New York or fighting off Indians and rattlesnakes in Indiana; they saw only the wives of merchant marine captains. It was hard not to feel a twinge of envy for those wives, for the captain of a large merchant ship was as wealthy as the most successful doctors and lawyers ashore, and he and his family lived accordingly.

In the great days of American sailing ships, it was the rule rather than the exception for the captain to take his family to sea with him. If that was his desire, no one but his wife could overrule him because he was no mere employee of a shipping company but a part owner of the vessel. Furthermore, the other owners preferred having a good family man to look after their interests. A man with domestic ties was more content and more dependable. He was less likely than a rootless bachelor to overindulge in drink or to forget his responsibilities in the lure of some South Sea isle — at least when his good wife was with him. The owners also agreed that the quarters provided for the captain at sea should be suitable to his station. It would reflect badly on the ship and on the American flag she flew if her officers did not enjoy the luxuries appropriate to the upper class. Understandably, women who might hesitate to follow their husbands to sea aboard a whaler were eager to embark as first lady aboard a merchant vessel.

By 1830 it seemed that anyone of consequence in a New England seaport town had been around the world at least once. An English visitor wrote of the people of Salem, Massachusetts, in 1834: "They speak of Fayal and the Azores as if they were close at hand. The fruits of the Mediterranean are on every table. They have a large acquaintance at Cairo. They know Napoleon's grave at St. Helena, and have wild tales to tell of Mozambique and Madagascar, and stores of ivory to show from there. They speak of the power of the king of Muscat, and are sensible of the riches of the southeast coast of Arabia. Anybody will give you anecdotes from Canton and descriptions of the Society and Sandwich Islands. They often slip up the western coast of their two continents, bringing furs from the back regions of their own wide land, glance up at the Andes on their return; double Cape Horn, touch at the ports of Brazil and Guiana, look about them in the West Indies, feeling almost at home there, and land some fair morning in Salem and walk home as if they had done nothing remarkable."

At sea the captain's family lived in what was known as the after cabin and took its meals in the forward cabin. Although there were differences between ships and a few changes in design as the nineteenth century wore on, the accommodations were much the same in their essential features. The after cabin was entered by a companionway, a short flight of stairs. There were small square windows all around, which were protected by heavy shutters that could be closed in bad weather and a large, raised skylight in the center. At night, light was provided by swinging whale-oil or kerosene lamps. The captain's stateroom was in one corner; another corner held the bathroom and toilet, which drew water from two tanks that offered a choice of salt or fresh. The bathroom also contained the ship's medicine chest, which was stocked with everything from castor oil to morphine. The remaining two corners held two more staterooms, leaving a cross-shaped area in the center of the after cabin known as the main saloon. The alcoves at the sides were fitted with built-in sofas, ornately carved and richly upholstered, and a sideboard was built between the two doors that led to the forward cabin. A few easy chairs and a table completed the furnishing of the after cabin.

When the ship was under way, the parlor had the clean, stripped-down appearance implied by the term *shipshape*. All the furniture was bolted down, expensive carpets that could not stand an accidental wetting with seawater were stowed away, and the great clutter of knickknacks was packed up. But whenever the ship dropped anchor, the captain's wife put things to rights again according to her own standards. Out came tablecloths and doilies, music boxes and china tea sets, quantities of photographs in fancy frames, until the main saloon was transformed into a typical Victorian parlor, where the captain's wife would entertain the other ladies in port at elegant tea parties.

The forward cabin was a long, narrow room, lighted by a skylight, with the pantry and staterooms opening off its sides. A long table, designed with racks to keep dishes from sliding off, filled the center. Settees made of mahogany or teak were screwed to the deck on each side and a revolving armchair, reserved for the captain, was fastened at the head. The staterooms in the forward cabin were for the mates and the steward and stewardess, if one was aboard. The cook, carpenter, and other privileged members of the crew had special quarters forward, while the common sailors were berthed as far as possible from the captain, at the forward end of the ship.

Although the space provided for the ship's "royal family" was small, it was as luxurious as money and skill could make it. Both cabins were finished by expert cabinetmakers, decorated with carvings, and trimmed with gold leaf or precious woods. Some even had stained-

glass windows behind the built-in sofas. And there were
advantages to small quarters, which women were more
likely to appreciate than men. Housekeeping was enor-
mously simplified. The convenience of disposing of gar-
bage and trash by heaving it over the side could not be
duplicated on shore. "Years after she had left the sea
and had lived on the prairies of Illinois for twenty-five
years," wrote a man who had grown up on ships, "I
heard my mother say that the thing she most missed
about her home at sea was having no 'overboard' at
hand."

Upper-class women, who had a staff of servants to
help run the mansions wealthy Americans might have
on shore, constantly worried about shopping, cleaning,
and disciplining servants and children, who could easily
get into trouble simply by walking out the back door
into a world full of temptations. Even social obligations
were less burdensome; no one expected a woman who
lived on a ship to give a large sit-down dinner, and it
was not necessary to pay duty calls on people one did
not like when home was on the open sea. No wonder
that the journals of merchant captains' wives often reflect a happiness bordering on euphoria. "It seems to
me I never was more blest than at the present," wrote
Hannah Burgess on her first voyage with her husband.
"The *Whirlwind* is a first-rate sailing ship . . . We have
an excellent steward. He cooks better than I can, I am
confident. The ship is supplied with provisions of every
kind, and I am enjoying myself as well as any person

can who has their husband's society and everything else convenient and comfortable."

The reference to the steward is significant, because the presence of such captains' servants, who were subject to shipboard discipline and could not quit, relieved the captain's lady of almost all work and most of her domestic worries. Women might do a little dusting in the after cabin and wash out their own lingerie, but the cabin boy did the regular family laundry, the steward did the heavy cleaning, sweeping, and polishing, and the cook prepared the family meals. Among the other comforts merchant marine wives might enjoy was the presence of a female among the captain's servants, a stewardess — usually the wife of one of the crew — who was particularly helpful when a woman expected to be delivered of a child at sea or had a number of small children traveling with her. Stewardesses enjoyed considerable prestige in comparison to other domestic servants of the period, and earned good pay. Some of them were paid a salary almost as high as that of the first officer.

The meals at the captain's table were as luxurious as it was possible to make them, given the lack of refrigeration. Unless there was a goat on board, the only milk they had was condensed, from a can. Tinned butter was also available, but in tropical climates it was soft and oily even when it did not go rancid. But anything that could be kept in good condition by their limited methods of food preservation would be taken aboard if the captain's family fancied it: clams, oysters, salmon, lobster, deviled ham, turkey, chicken, ox tongue, sausage, frankfurters, rabbit, roast beef, roast veal, mutton, tomatoes, sweet potatoes, corn, peas, string beans, lima beans, beets, spinach, asparagus, onions, and canned fruits. Live chickens and pigs supplemented the diet as did such delicacies from the sea as dolphin and porpoise. Flying fish were said to be delicious and any that landed on the deck were, by custom, reserved for the captain's wife — unless the ship's cat got to them first.

Food shortages might develop on a long voyage. Sometimes provisions went bad because of the activity of mice, rats, weevils, and cockroaches. When the supply of luxury foodstuffs was depleted, the captain's family had to eat salt beef from the crew's stores. The family always got the best pieces, however, and food damaged by vermin was still considered good enough to feed to the sailors. Running short of fresh vegetables, or having the potatoes and onions go bad, was the greatest hardship those who dined in the cabin were apt to endure, and as soon as they reached port boats would swarm from shore, loaded with goods the captain could buy: milk, meat, vegetables, coconuts, bananas in the Pacific, peaches and grapes in Chile, litchi nuts and sweet oranges in China.

Food in the forecastle was much different. On a good ship the sailors would not go hungry, but their stomachs were filled mostly with salt meat and hard bread, pea soup and baked beans. Treats consisted of rice and molasses or a stiff flour pudding called duff. Duff was supposed to have raisins in it, but these were added very sparingly. Of course, if the captain retained a taste for duff from his days of sailing before the mast, the pudding would appear at cabin meals, liberally seeded with raisins, and with citron as well.

It is difficult for people today to appreciate how thirty or so people, confined together for several months in a ship at sea, could accept the extreme social stratification that was taken for granted in the great age of sailing ships. The captain and his wife and children were the royal family of a tiny, but very wealthy, kingdom. The mates and the captain's servants were members of the royal household, and most of them shipped out with the captain again and again, staying with him for many years. Before maritime workers were unionized, however, members of the crew were virtual slaves; they were brought on board by force, rarely collected the wages due them, and were treated like brute animals. They were quickly forgotten when the ship made port somewhere after a few months at sea, and they fled to shore to be replaced by new hands, equally brutalized and degraded.

The crews of American merchant ships had not always been made up of the polyglot mixture of rootless laborers that came to be known as "packet rats." In the eighteenth century, ambitious New England boys began a seafaring career by shipping before the mast and a good proportion gradually worked their way up to captain. The Napoleonic wars brought increasing numbers of foreigners, who were easily exploited, into the U.S.

Merchant Marine. At the same time the Industrial Revolution offered many more opportunities to ambitious boys, and the increasing demands for speed — which necessitated carrying more sail — made sailors' work harder and more dangerous than it had ever been before. Although many commanders of merchant ships in the nineteenth century had once been foremast hands, they found fewer and fewer men like themselves in their crews. Those who anticipated a future at sea usually enlisted as cabin boys, to gain the special social status that position conferred.

Fred B. Duncan, who went to sea as a boy with his mother and four brothers and sisters aboard the merchant ship *Florence,* recalled anxiously watching the boarding of the crew. Sixteen of them were to join the captain, his family, two mates, the bosun, carpenter, steward, cook, and cabin boy, and they came from many nations. He remembered a time "we had a huge, gorilla-like man who could neither understand nor talk to anyone aboard, although we had speakers of many tongues that voyage." When they came aboard, however, no one knew what language they spoke, because they were usually unconscious. They had been made drunk or drugged by sailors' boardinghouse keepers, who had "helped" them discharge their debts for lodging and liquor by signing on for a voyage. They were brought out to the ship while she was anchored in the harbor. "This prevented the escape of anyone who might experience a sudden change of mind when he sobered up and realized . . . that he had signed his name or made his mark to the ship's articles and was bound to her for the duration of a voyage that might last for many months," Duncan explained. They were searched for weapons, and when they woke were subjected to a period of what Duncan called "shaking down and readjustment."

The men who had never been to sea before were too seasick or frightened to go aloft and handle sail. Those wise in the ways of ships were determined to do no more work than they had to. "Ship, crew, and officers were trying each other out," as Duncan put it. Officers dealt with the language barrier and what they saw as the stupidity or malingering of sailors in a simple, straightforward manner. Those who failed to do as they were told promptly and well were beaten — with bare fists and feet by officers strong enough to win in a fair fight or with brass knuckles or a belaying pin by officers who needed some help in enforcing their authority. Within a week or two, the crew was working twelve hours a day in four-hour shifts, so the men never got a full night's sleep; they lived in unheated vermin-infested quarters and ate what they were served, obeying the regulation that they do all their grumbling where no officer could hear it. The captain, of course, had to deal with these men, but his wife and children were supposed to do their best to ignore their existence.

That was easier said than done, especially for the children, who could not reasonably be expected to confine their movements to the cabin for months on end. Once allowed on deck the little ones and the sailors would see each other, and the most sullen member of the crew could rarely resist the happy, curious children. Sailors were not allowed to talk to the children, but they could smile at them and watch them play. On one ship the children were permitted to wave to sailors who stayed with the crew for more than one voyage. So these lonely, homeless men often spent their free hours making little gifts for the captain's offspring. Duncan remembers his sister treasuring a wooden doll, and his receiving at Christmas time "odd packages, clumsily wrapped and smelling of snuff and tobacco."

In addition, children were permitted to talk to the officers who dined at the captain's table, to the captain's servants, and perhaps to such superior members of the crew as the sailmaker and carpenter. Joanna Carver Colcord, who was born at sea and spent most of her childhood aboard her father's ship, recalled the visits she and her younger brother Linc were permitted to make to the Chinese cook. They must not disturb him while he was working, but they went to the galley "after the day's dinner was over and before he retired to smoke, with great decorum, his daily pipeful of opium." That was a fairly conventional addiction. Fred Duncan recalled the first mate of the *Florence* indulging a craving for castor oil, which he would sip slowly, "with the relish of a connoisseur who is tasting a rare vintage," as the boy watched. "After all these years," Duncan wrote, "I still sicken at the memory."

With so much assistance in keeping an eye on their children and the limited opportunities for mischief available on a merchant ship, mothers in the merchant marine probably had an easier time in many respects than mothers on shore. Children born and raised at sea seem to have been unusually healthy, perhaps because they were isolated from other children for long periods and thus protected from such deadly childhood diseases as diphtheria. Childbirth at sea, from the statistics available, also seems to have been less dangerous, perhaps because the mother was protected from the excessive attentions of male doctors who, until well into the nineteenth century, did not understand that their unwashed hands could transmit diseases. Women who expected to go into labor at sea might make special arrangements. A midwife known as Grandma Searle, from the seafaring town of Searsport, Maine, made a career for herself by going to sea with pregnant women and delivering their babies. Stewardesses could also come in handy as midwives. Most women relied on their husbands' help when their time came, because the captain usually acted as ship's doctor.

But captains had other duties, and babies sometimes chose the most inconvenient times to make their appearance. Joanna Carver Colcord's little brother was born just after the ship, leaking badly, had rounded Cape Horn, one of the most difficult passages in the world, and the wind was still blowing a gale. When Joanna had been born the year before, her mother had Grandma Searle aboard; but this time the captain had midwife duty in addition to dealing with wind tearing at his sails and water rising below decks.

Captains, however, were generally proud of their ability to deal coolly and competently with any earthly emergency. Captain Samuels, recording the birth of a daughter at four o'clock one morning on the cargo ship *Manhattan,* observed, "A ship-master is called upon to act many parts in the drama of life, and if he is a thorough sailor he acts well in every emergency." Of course, little Miss Samuels had had the grace to arrive in good weather: "The sea was smooth as glass, with light airs and calms; the only squall we knew was from the young mermaid."

Seafaring children who grew up on merchant vessels seem to have enjoyed the life as much as their mothers did. Joanna Carver Colcord found young seafaring friends all over the world, in every port her father's ship visited. Many had been born at sea as she had and were christened with odd names in recognition of the places near which they had been born, such as Fastnet, Iona, and Mindoro. Joanna had been born near the French penal colony of New Caledonia and was very glad her parents had not decided to name her for that island.

Captains' children also found playmates among the natives of their ports of call. Colcord remembered playing with "the Chinese youngsters without a word of common language." They "swapped cake and candy for gaudy paper lanterns, fished, and had a generally gorgeous time." She remembered nights when she visited with her family aboard other ships, where she "listened to marvelous stories from the world's best raconteurs — seamen — and agonized in the vain effort to stay awake to hear the end of the last and most enthralling tale."

She remembered peddlers who visited the ship and spread their wares on the deck for the captain's wife to inspect: lacquered pieces, embroidery, and jewelry. Once, on her birthday, a peddler unwrapped a knotted rag bundle of moonstones and allowed the girl to pick one as a gift. Even more exciting were visits from magicians: "They would squat upon their squares of cloth spread upon the deck, plant the mango seed in front of them and make it grow before our wondering eyes. They would plunge the sword through the basket in which we had *seen* the little boy tied up and packed away — but always, when the horror was getting too great to bear, he would come running unharmed from the shelter of the cabin."

Colcord returned from her last voyage in 1900, when she was eighteen and about to go to college. "I remember thinking," she later recalled, "with the cherished sadness of youth, as I went down the gangplank and out into South Street, 'The happiest days of my life are forever behind me.' "

Children were encouraged to write letters and keep journals at sea, and many families today possess records documenting the adventures of grandmothers or great-grandmothers who traveled the world with the merchant marine when they were girls. Some of these children's diaries are preserved in museums, and a few have been published in whole or in part. Among the most charming is that of Alice Rowe Snow, which was published under the title *Log of a Sea Captain's Daughter* forty years ago.

Alice Rowe, as she was known before her marriage, went to sea for the first time at the age of eleven months on her father's ship, *Village Belle*. She learned to walk on the rolling deck on that voyage, and when she made her first attempts to walk on a stationary floor she could not manage it and cried out in terror. Alice Rowe did not spend all of her early years at sea, however; there was a year on a banana plantation in Santo Domingo and another period when her father was in business in Liverpool, England. But in 1883, when Alice Rowe was fourteen, her father took command of the *Russell*, and the family embarked on a voyage that would last four and a half years.

From the beginning, Alice Rowe was enthusiastic. "I feel so happy," the diary begins, "I just want to shout right out and tell everybody that I am going on a long sea voyage with Father and Mother. All the boys and girls I know think I am lucky and want to come, too. I wish they could, but of course they can't. Although I am only a little girl, I will write a book all by myself and make pictures, too. Then when I come home my boy and girl friends can find out what I have been doing. I wonder, oh, how I wonder what will be written in this book!" It turned out that one of her boy friends had come along as a stowaway; Harry Kidd was allowed to remain as cabin boy and share in the adventures, of which there were plenty. The one that made the greatest impression on Alice Rowe was a stop at Robinson Crusoe's island in the South Pacific.

Even in quiet times, when there were no adventures,

the captain's family enjoyed life at sea. Some pastimes were identical to those that upper-middle-class women might indulge in at home. Elizabeth G. B. Barrett wrote poetry that was good enough to be published; it suited Victorian tastes, and the act of capturing her emotions in verse clearly gave her the same sort of pleasure that making journal entries gave less talented women:

> *Far out: there's not a sail in sight;*
> *We are alone upon the deep;*
> *And now my heart grows strangely light,*
> *As if with wild, unfettered sweep*
> *'T would pierce that glorious air, as now*
> *Our vessel cleaves this surging tide,*
> *And like the foam-flakes from our prow,*
> *Fling all earth's petty cares aside;*
> *'T is joy to think that I am free*
> *As these wild winds far out at sea.*

Emma Gray, another cultured woman, had a piano aboard the *Fire Queen* and composed music while she was at sea. Emma Gray also enjoyed embroidery.

Needlework was a popular pastime at sea for the captains as well as their wives. Scrimshaw was a craft practiced only on whalers, which had a plentiful supply of ivory and bone. In the merchant marine, captains made net lace and did needlepoint as well as indulged in such better-known hobbies as making ship models of wood and scrap materials. Captain Josiah Knowles made a doll house for his daughter while he was in command of the *Charger*. It was an exact scale model of his home on

Cape Cod, and he furnished it with miniatures he bought in England.

One new handcraft was developed by women of the merchant marine when hundreds of ships began calling at islands off the coast of Peru to collect guano — bird droppings — which was much in demand as fertilizer in the 1860s and 1870s. No one lived on these islands and there was nothing to do on shore during the months a ship might be anchored there but watch the birds produce the only export. Finally a captain's wife noticed the many varieties of seaweed and discovered that they could be floated on paper and arranged in multicolored designs. These would stick permanently when they were dry because of the surface gelatin in the plants. Making Chincha Island sea moss pictures was quite a fad for a while. As late as the 1890s, a girl who went to sea with her grandmother on the clipper ship *Glory of the Seas* observed "Tooty" spending long days clipping and arranging bits of maroon, green, black, and yellow seaweed to make trees and wreaths on five-inch-square pieces of white cardboard.

From the captain's standpoint, one of the chief advantages of having his wife and children accompany him to sea was that he could enjoy the same sorts of amusements he did at home. The social stratification believed to be indispensable at sea forbade the captain from socializing even with his officers. But with his wife on board, there were evenings of reading aloud or playing dominoes, cribbage, or poker. Tooty taught her granddaughter, when she was seven, to play poker. Perhaps she was hoping to liven up the games; Tooty regularly beat the captain when they played.

Although children had a good time at sea, they were not as free as children on land to choose their activities. The most important rule they had to obey was to be quiet while people were trying to sleep, which at sea was most of the time. The system of watches — four hours on duty followed by four hours off — meant that except for the first dogwatch (the period from 4:00 to 6:00 P.M., when the watch was split so that the same people would not have to do the least pleasant midnight to 4:00 A.M. shift every day) and mealtimes, one of the mates was always trying to sleep in his stateroom in the forward cabin. That sleep was precious to him and important to the safety of the ship. Children, therefore, must make absolutely no unnecessary noise, and their quiet games on deck had to be played on the side opposite that occupied by the sleeping officer's stateroom. Quiet games did not mean simply no running and yelling; they had to be played without talking. If children used hand signals rather than words, they could play such card games as Authors. A popular diversion involved navigation charts and dominoes. The dominoes, in imagination, were ships that loaded cargo and sailed from port to port with perhaps a shipwreck or an encounter with Chinese pirates to liven things up. Children might also be caught up in an adult hobby like building ship models in whiskey bottles.

Days were not filled with games for children at sea, however. They spent as much time on lessons as children at home. Seafaring parents took education seriously, and the mother presided over regular school lessons based on the books and examinations used by the children at home. Joanna Carver Colcord realized she was handicapped in studying languages and science, which were not her mother's specialty. Still, she was able to keep up with her contemporaries on shore. Her final high school examinations were sent out from Searsport High School, and she took them, under her mother's supervision, while they were anchored in Hong Kong harbor. Six months later she picked up her diploma in Searsport.

Reading is perhaps the most enjoyable of all quiet pastimes, and children at sea generally liked to read. Unfortunately, their choice of literature was restricted to what happened to be on board. The captain's family might take with them a limited number of books and magazines, which they would trade with other families they met in port. There was also a ship's library, provided by the charitable people who supported the American Seamen's Friend Society. The volumes ran heavily to religious tracts, hymnbooks, and the least popular books from secondhand shops. One girl recalled such typical titles as *The Care and Feeding of Pedigree Dogs* and *The Modern Science of Surgery*. Joanna Carver Colcord remembered studying volumes of sailing directions when nothing else was left on board that she had not already read.

In the late afternoon, when lessons were over and everyone was awake in the dogwatch, noisy play was permitted. The children on the *Florence* had wagons and tricycles, and a baby carriage was aboard for giving the youngest an airing. These wheeled vehicles presented a special challenge on a rolling deck. Fred Duncan recalled: "After school we rode them about the deck as long as twilight lasted. If there was wind enough to give the deck a slant it took skill to ride a three-wheeler successfully." The Duncan family also had a sort of swimming pool on deck. Made of canvas, it was about ten feet square and four feet deep and reserved for the exclusive use of the captain's family. They would all troop out together to go bathing, dressed in the thoroughly modest bathing suits of the 1890s.

Although children raised at sea had experiences in common with those raised on land in the Victorian era, they learned something more from their special upbringing. The many places they visited and the unusual sights they saw colored their thinking for the rest of their lives. But they also learned certain rules for living from their days at sea. "We learned sterner things," Joanna Carver Colcord recalled, "instant obedience, orderliness, a necessary quality in the close confines of a ship, contempt for sham and double dealing because you cannot fool the sea. We learned that a job must be well done for its own sake, with that little extra touch for good measure that is implied in the word shipshape. And we learned something of the inexorability of duty, stern taskmaster of all our days."

Children had duties aboard the merchant ships because their parents had no intention of raising offspring who did not understand the importance of work. After all, although ships' captains might be wealthy men, they had earned their money in a hard trade. Because it was what they knew, they taught their children about the work of the ship. Both boys and girls learned to read the compass, sight the sun, and steer. Joanna Carver Colcord and her brother were also made responsible for the ship's signal flags, selecting the proper code ensigns to be hoisted to transmit a message to another ship and translating the reply.

As children grew older, however, distinctions between boys and girls became more important to their parents and different rules were applied to them. Although neither boys nor girls were ever supposed to go on deck forward of the mainmast, which was strictly sailors' territory, boys might occasionally sneak over anyway. As girls grew older, their range on the deck was increasingly restricted and the ban on passing signs of recognition with any member of the crew more rigidly enforced. Boys were permitted, even encouraged, to climb the rigging, while girls were forbidden to do so. Joanna Carver Colcord resented these restrictions and was irked at being told to behave "like a little lady" and forced to learn to sew while her brother had the freedom of the deck. But she did as she was told; like everyone else, she obeyed the captain.

A few captain fathers, particularly those who were not doing too well financially, had different ideas about their daughters. Some deliberately made sailors out of them, deciding that they needed a reliable crew aboard more than a little lady. Ladies, after all, are a luxury that not everyone can afford. Annie Slade, who was born in England in 1865 and had a long career at sea, first served under her father, quitting school to go aboard the *Dahlia*. She learned how to steer by the compass, how to trim the sails, and the land and tides of the coasts the *Dahlia* traveled. She also learned to predict the weather. As soon as she knew enough, her father made her mate — in charge of the watch while he slept. The *Dahlia* was a leaky craft and needed constant pumping at sea. "Often I have heard mother talk of the hours she stood at the pumps in her high laced-up boots with hardly any time to rest or make a cup of tea till she eventually arrived at the port of discharge," her son recalled. In addition to these duties, the captain's daughter cooked for her father and the crew.

Thirty-five years before Annie Slade was born, another seafaring daughter herself became a captain in the merchant marine. A Glasgow newspaper of 1852 made note of "an heroic and exceedingly clever young lady, Miss Betsy Miller, daughter of the late Mr. W. Miller." The late Mr. Miller owned several ships in the coasting trade both in Great Britain and the United States. His daughter had worked as "ship's husband" for him and he finally gave her command of the *Cloetus*. At the time the newspaper account appeared, the "young lady" had been captain of the *Cloetus* for more than twenty years, "and she has weathered the storms of the deep when many commanders of the other sex have been driven to pieces on the rocks."

Except for captains' daughters, who had special advantages, women, before the twentieth century, were strongly discouraged from enlisting in the merchant marine as anything but stewardesses.

A case brought before the High Court of Admiralty in England in 1821, however, elicited a ruling that "sex alone does not create a legal or total disqualification." The case involved one Elizabeth Stephens, who sued the captain of the *Jane and Matilda* for wages due her for three voyages she made between England and Spain. She had signed on as cook and steward, but witnesses testified that she was "robust in body and limb and exhibited great skill and strength." More to the point, she did the work of an able-bodied seaman; she "stood watches, took her turn at the helm and hauled ropes on deck," and it was for these tasks that she demanded back pay. The court did not render its decision in favor of Stephens very graciously. More than a year and a half after the case was filed, Lord Stowell found in her favor only after deploring "a woman doing man's work on board ship as it could lead to moral disorder," at the same time assuming that the "disorder" must have existed: "I suspect the captain engaged the services of this woman in more capacities than those described . . . did she act in character of his wife, or in a less honorable connection?" One wonders whether His Lordship believed the activities of an able-bodied seaman to be more or less honorable than those of a wife.

At any rate, before this century any woman who had serious ambitions for a career as a sailor and was not related to the owner had little chance of succeeding unless she could disguise her sex, which some did. One Rebecca Anne Johnson was discovered to be a female in 1808 after she served for seven years on the crew of an English coal ship. Perhaps she had inherited a talent for disguising her sex as well as her taste for seafaring; her mother had died during the Napoleonic Wars while serving with a gun crew aboard a warship.

Another case, which came to the attention of the Lord Mayor of London in 1835, involved sixteen-year-old Ann Jane Thornton. She had signed on the *Sarah* for a voyage from the United States. The captain said that when she signed the articles she was dressed as a sailor and looked like one. A few days before the ship arrived in London, her sex was revealed when some of the crew watched as she washed herself in her berth. They had already suspected she wasn't a real man, the captain said, because she refused to drink grog. But she did the work of a seaman; the captain said, "She would run up to hand the topgallant sail in any sort of weather and they had had a severe passage. She had had a hard time, suffering greatly from the wet, but she had borne it all excellently and was a capital seaman." Not all of the crew agreed with the captain. Ann Jane Thornton testified that "during the voyage she had been struck by some of the sailors because she could not work as hard as they did — a thing she found difficult to do in a gale, but she had not complained as she was determined to endure as much as possible without grumbling."

Pressed for details of her history by the Lord Mayor,

she revealed that she had been at sea for three years,
first shipping out at the age of thirteen as a cabin boy.
She signed on to get free passage to New York, to meet
a man to whom she had "become strongly attached."
When she reached New York she learned that the man
she was seeking had died a few days earlier. So she
signed on as cook and steward, first in the *Adelaide* and
then in the *Sarah*, where her sex was finally discovered.
What became of this young woman after these adventures is unknown. The Lord Mayor gave her some
money to pay her passage home; perhaps that is where
she went.

Ann Jane Thornton's decision to go to sea as a cabin
boy was hardly commonplace, but the relative ease with
which a teenaged girl could pass herself off as a boy
made it feasible. Like the women masquerading as men
who served aboard warships, the memory of the few who
did so was preserved in the folk wisdom of popular
songs. One with a novel twist involves the "Handsome
Cabin Boy," who attracted both the captain of a trading
vessel and the captain's wife:

'Tis of a handsome female as you may understand
Her mind being bent in rambling unto some foreign land
She dressed herself in sailor's clothes, or so it does appear,
And hired with our captain to serve him for a year.

The captain's wife she being on board, she seemed in great joy,
To see her husband had engaged such a handsome cabin boy
And now and then she'd slip in a kiss, and she would have liked
*   to toy,*

*But it was the captain found out the secret of the handsome cabin
    boy.*

His cheeks were red and rosy and his hair hung in its curls,
The sailors often smiled and said he looks just like a girl.
But eating the captain's biscuits, their color didn't destroy,
And the waist did swell on pretty Nell, the handsome cabin boy.

'Twas in the Bay of Biscay our gallant ship did plow,
One night among the sailors was a fearful scurrying row.
They tumbled from their hammocks, for their sleep it did destroy,
And swore about the groaning of the handsome cabin boy.

"Oh, doctor, dear doctor," the cabin boy did cry,
"My time has come, I am undone and I must surely die."
The doctor came a-running and he smiled at the fun,
To think a sailor lad should have a daughter or a son.

*The sailors, when they heard the joke, they all did stand and
    stare.*
The child belonged to none of them, they solemnly did swear.
The captain's wife she looked at him and said, "I wish you joy,
For it's either you or I betrayed the handsome cabin boy."

Then each man took his tot of rum, and drunk success to trade,
And likewise to the cabin boy, who was neither man nor maid.
Here's hoping the wars don't rise again, our sailors to destroy
*And here's hoping for a jolly lot more like the handsome cabin
    boy.*

Pregnancy was definitely out of the question for
women who hoped to rise in the merchant marine in
male disguise. It was, we can be sure, only by sacrificing
a normal sexual life that the woman serving as second
officer of an American ship, when her secret was con-

fided to a writer in 1908, was able to keep her job. And the same may be said of Captain John Weed, "who had commanded transatlantic vessels for many years," and whose sex was discovered only after "he" committed suicide in a home for old sailors in 1905.

By far the easiest and most satisfying way for a woman to go to sea before the present century was as the captain's wife. As such she could enjoy the travel and, if she wished, do the work of an officer. Occasionally she might sign the articles and get paid; if not, she had a legal right to share in her husband's income, which she would have the satisfaction of seeing grow through her efforts. Of course, if she was ambitious for command, she would do best to choose a man who was not too well off to begin with; the higher a man's social standing in the nineteenth century, the more determined he usually was not to be "shamed" by having a working wife.

Annie Slade, the English woman who first went to sea as a captain's daughter, is typical of many working women from seaport towns in the last part of the nineteenth century. They helped their husbands build a family fortune, lifting them from near poverty into the ranks of the middle class. Annie married W. K. Slade while he was mate of a vessel called the *Hawk*. He was an ambitious man and a hard worker, but he was illiterate and could not even read a navigation chart. His wife undertook to educate him, and he made enough progress to be offered a position as master of the *Francis Beddoe*. "He naturally talked it over with mother," their son recorded, "and it was agreed that he could do the job and of course the business part fell to her."

She went with him on the *Francis Beddoe* as navigator and business manager, taking charge of all the money. Soon the Slades had both a savings account and a baby. When the child was three months old, Annie Slade took him and went back to sea again, taking a turn at watches as well as continuing her other duties and caring for the infant. Meanwhile Captain Slade was given command of slightly larger ships. Finally, Annie Slade counted up what was in the bank and found they had enough to buy a quarter share of the *Alpha*. Now the family was really on its way because a quarter of the profits of each voyage, as well as wages, went to Captain Slade. At the same time their family was growing, and Annie Slade took several children with her when she sailed in the *Alpha*. There, her son recalled, "She did the cooking which was pleasing to the crew, and always scrubbed the cabin out. At sea she took a spell at the wheel whenever required. If father was ever shorthanded, she filled the vacancy most efficiently." Once, when Captain Slade sailed without her, his crew left him, and he sent his wife a telegram asking her to send him a mate. She couldn't find anyone to take the job, so she got on a train, met him in port where he was taking on a load of coal, and took the mate's job herself.

Of course, Annie Slade observed the conventions of her times and never expected recognition for her work. But her husband and children appreciated her nonetheless. When she discussed the family business, she "did not make anything of her own part in the fight for survival," her son wrote. "Everything that happened was due to father's ability but as time passed by, we all got to understand how much mother did for him. Perhaps as eldest son who sailed with him I had a better understanding than anyone else and a better reason to appreciate what part of his success was due to his wife and her ability." What seemed to impress the younger Slade most about his mother's activity at sea was not that she was a woman doing a sailor's work but that she did it without coming from a seafaring family. True, her father had been a captain, but her uncles were soldiers. "All but one were regimental sergeant majors and saw service all over the world during the reign of Queen Victoria," he wrote. "In these circumstances it seems marvellous to me that mother took to the sea like a duck takes to water." And there was no question that she had the instincts for wind and weather that no amount of study can instill and that seafaring people often assumed must be inherited, like keen eyes or good teeth.

Her son recalled an occasion on the *Alpha* when something in the atmosphere struck Annie Slade as not right. She had been asleep but it woke her and she went on deck. After watching the sails for a few minutes she decided the captain was carrying too much canvas. "At last she said, 'You are driving the ship too heavy, if you don't take the topsail in, you'll lose the lot.' Father just laughed at her in a patronizing way and said, 'She'll carry it or drag it and I'll be in Waterford tonight.' Well, mother was right. She put us boys down in father's bunk and up she went on deck again. She had only just got up when topmast, topsail, yard and flying jib, all came tumbling down in a tangle. I heard mother shouting, saying 'I told you so. Now you can go up and clear that lot away, I'll take the wheel.' 'All right,' he said, 'I'll soon secure that. Keep her on course, we won't be long.' " But it took quite a while, and the children had a few peeks from the cabin. Of this incident the oldest son wrote, "What I've wondered many times since is that mother stood there so unperturbed doing a man's job that seemed to come so naturally to her, seeing her antecedents were not born close to the sea."

For relatives of the master of a small coasting vessel to go to sea as working members of the crew was fairly common in the United States as well as in Britain. It was a way to save wages, and the tradition of marriage as a working partnership was slower to die out among poorer families than among the wealthy. For a wife to work as a sailor on her husband's ship or even to take command of a vessel he owned was probably safer and more profitable for the family than to have her take in laundry or toil in a textile mill. Like Annie Slade, however, these working women did not think of themselves as doing anything remarkable; and so their stories are preserved mainly as oral traditions by their descendants.

At least one nineteenth-century captain transported cargoes along the New England coast in his forty-one-ton vessel with no assistance at all except from his wife and their fifteen-year-old son. No written record of this practice on the *Rockaway* would have been preserved had the ship not run into trouble on Christmas Eve in the year 1883. Unable to make harbor in a blinding snowstorm, the captain anchored just north of Rye Beach, New Hampshire, and hoisted a distress signal. The three were rescued by the Life Saving Service at the Rye station and the incident written up in the Life Saving Service annual report, whose authors thought finding a family working as crew most unusual. Or perhaps they wondered that three people of any sort would be at sea during a gale on Christmas Eve.

Wives who worked at sea were more likely to fill an officer's slot than to serve as sailors. The amount of authority a woman was permitted to assume depended on the informal power relationship she negotiated with her husband, which has always been different with every marriage and has relatively little to do with either law or contemporary custom. It is a matter of personal relations. Some husbands wanted no advice or help from their wives, even though their wives were competent and offered it. Captain John G. Pendleton is an example of that type. He was captain and owner of the *William H. Connor*, and his determination to make top speed in any weather gave him a reputation as a "canvas spreader" or "kite flyer" because of the amount of sail he carried. His wife, Sarah, knew a good deal about ships and the sea, and on their honeymoon cruise she grew concerned about the sails and went to the quarterdeck to tell him about it. While they were discussing the matter, the main topgallant sail blew out of the bolt ropes and disappeared downwind. The captain's comment was, "Well, my dear, there's one sail we don't need worry about," but as soon as she went below he had a new main topgallant set. So much for good advice. Eventually, Captain Pendleton lost a ship with all hands at sea, drowning at the age of twenty-seven.

In contrast was the situation aboard the *Hampton Westcott*, when Samuel Samuels first went to sea as a cabin boy. Both the captain and the mate had brought their wives with them. "I soon saw who the real captain and mate were," Samuels recalled. The captain's wife handled ropes and relieved her husband at the helm, and the mate's wife was as ready to enforce discipline as any man. "She was a muscular woman," Samuels remembered, "and seizing a belaying-pin, she used it with the skill of a Liverpool packet-mate" on a sailor who had played a nasty practical joke on the greenhorn cabin boy.

Even a captain's wife who did not involve herself in the day-to-day operations of the ship was expected to make herself useful in an emergency. Helpless, hysterical women were not considered charming, even in the Victorian age, when there was real danger. Captain Thomas Crapo was so proud of his wife's seafaring abilities that he wrote a whole book, in which she got equal billing, of their adventures together. He published it under the title *Strange, But True: Life and Adventures of Captain Crapo and Wife*. An example of her coolness was her quick action to provide light for the compass box after an accident aboard the American brig *Kaluna*, when her husband was first mate. "Besides smashing our boat it stove in the cabin and started it from the deck and filled it more than half full of water. My wife was the only woman on board and the only occupant of the cabin at the time. And she, instead of fainting as many men would have done at such a time, grasped the lamp from a socket and held it up to the binnacle [which] was smashed, lamp and all. Hers was not a very comfortable position, nearly waist deep in water holding up a lamp so the helmsman could see how to steer. That was a good sign of presence of mind in an emergency. She knew as soon as the binnacle light went out something must be done to give those on deck light, and acted as stated above; and she was more than praised for her bravery."

Mutiny was a constant danger at sea in the nineteenth century; if it occurred, there were no noncombatants. The captain's wife knew which side she was on; in an uprising she could remain uninvolved only up to a point. As on the American frontier during the same years, women fought and killed when they had to. The *Frank N. Thayer* was headed back to New York from Manila with a load of hemp in January 1866, when two sailors who had joined the crew in the Pacific mutinied. They killed five men and wounded six others, including the captain's wife. Armed with knives and a harpoon, the two islanders held control of the ship for more than twenty-four hours. Then the captain and his wife, both armed with navy revolvers and assisted by loyal sailors, retook the ship. The mutineers set fire to the vessel and tried to escape on a raft. The captain and his wife had a difference of opinion as to what to do with the pair floating within easy gunshot range in the water beside the burning ship. "Don't kill those men," said the captain's wife. "Lower a boat and bring them aboard . . . Bring them aboard so we can hang them from the yardarm." But the captain's order was, "Finish them off quickly. Then all hands turn to for fire-fighting." It was, however, impossible to save the ship. The survivors of the mutiny, including the captain's wife and child, crowded into one small lifeboat, made a sail out of two blankets, and finally reached land after a week on the open sea.

Some wives in the merchant marine signed the ship's articles as officers. One wife, who was knowledgeable about navigation and ship's business in general, signed on as purser for a wage of a shilling a month. She inspected the ship before permitting her husband to accept the command, and approved it largely because she had always wanted "to have a ship with a chart house on the poop . . . so convenient to do my sewing in." Although many wives kept the ship's accounts, like the whalers' wives their most common area of expertise was navigation. Indeed, in many parts of New England navigation was considered a necessary part of a girl's education. For instance, Dukes County Academy on Martha's Vineyard advertised navigation as one of the subjects offered by its "female department" in the 1830s. In addition to drawing and painting, which were generally encouraged feminine "accomplishments," the acad-

emy gave "particular attention" to projection, drawing,
and coloring maps. When Samuel Samuels served aboard
the *Henry Pratt* as second mate on a transatlantic voyage, the captain's wife gave him lessons in navigation.
After her husband died, Samuels learned, this woman
established a school of navigation in London.

Navigation was an essential skill at sea. Hauling lines
and setting sail to keep the ship moving was important;
so was physical intimidation of the crew, who were always somewhat unwilling captives on a voyage. Yet unless someone aboard knew the ship's location and how
to plot a course to its destination, no amount of hauling
lines and cursing sailors would prevent catastrophe.
Thus, when a captain was disabled and his wife was the
best navigator on board, command of the ship would
most naturally fall to her. Mrs. Reed, the wife of the
captain of the *T. F. Oakes*, was not only a proficient
navigator but a better hand at the wheel than most of
the men aboard. The ship was in trouble in 1897, with
her husband sick, the first mate dead, and a good part
of the crew dead or dying of scurvy. She took command
and saved the ship. To honor her achievement the famous nautical insurers, Lloyd's of London, gave her
their prestigious Silver Medal.

Merchant ships came in many shapes and sizes and
sailed in many seas. Not all commands were equally
challenging. But certainly the most coveted of all in the
nineteenth century were the commands of the great
clipper ships, which vied with each other to set speed
records for the passage around Cape Horn to California

or China. Prices were always highest for the first ship to bring in the goods. Two women briefly commanded clippers before the end of the 1850s, the golden age of these swift, graceful ships. Both, of course, assumed command only in an emergency, because they were there when needed, and because they were captains' wives.

Hannah Burgess certainly never expected to take command of a clipper or even to go to sea with her husband when she married William Burgess in 1852. Indeed, she was seasick on her honeymoon during a short ferry trip between Boston and Cape Cod. The trip out was not too bad. "I was rather sick," she recorded in her journal, "but not having eaten any breakfast, I could not vomit. There were several ladies on board and we got along finely. First one would run to the closet and heave, then another. Real sport." After spending a fine day on Cape Cod, topped off by a banquet in Provincetown, the captain took his young bride home, again on the ferry — this trip was much worse. "I was so dizzy it took two or three men to steady me while reaching the settee," she wrote. "A gentleman wishing to do all he could for the afflicted gave me some brandy, which he said would ease me, and it did for I vomited quite well. Yes, lost all my nice dinner for which we paid $2."

William Burgess was about to take command of the clipper ship *Whirlwind*, which was still under construction on the day of his wedding. Three months later he was off to sea, and Hannah Burgess found the parting difficult. He was gone for a year, and on his next voyage his wife went to sea with him. And wonder of wonders — on the great ocean-going clipper, Hannah Burgess was not seasick at all! Hoping only to avoid the unhappiness the separation from her husband caused her, she discovered that seafaring life suited her marvelously well.

Within a few weeks at sea her journal took on a more businesslike form, recording the names of the officers and the number of men in the crew. She studied books on navigation and took lessons from her husband; after a month at sea the captain trusted her readings and calculations enough to turn over navigation of the *Whirlwind* entirely to her. She also "learned the ropes," so her journal contained such entries as, "At 2 P.M. word ship offshore, at 8 closereefed topsail, steered courses, at 9 P.M. took in fore and mizzen topsail, split the foretopmast staysail, unbent it and bent new one." The trickiest part of the voyage was always the westbound passage around Cape Horn, where gale-force winds fought the progress of the ship every mile of the way. Even then, Hannah Burgess did not complain of seasickness. Indeed, on one wild Sunday night when the force of the storm split a sail, she wrote, "I should liked to have been on deck then even though it meant being lashed to the rigging."

When, at the conclusion of this voyage, Captain Burgess was given command of an even larger clipper, the *Challenger*, there was no doubt that his wife would go to sea with him again. By this time she was a first-rate navigator. Her husband and every officer on the ship agreed that she was as good as the best captain sailing.

And Hannah Burgess adjusted quickly to the quirks of the new vessel. "I like the *Challenger* very much," she wrote. "She is a much better sailor than the *Whirlwind* and 400 tons larger." Just under eighteen months from the start of this voyage, on November 22, 1856, Captain Burgess became ill and was put to bed. He would never resume command.

With the captain incapacitated, Hannah Burgess and the first mate had a conference, and she agreed to navigate and take command of the ship. They headed for Valparaiso, the nearest port. For twenty days, Hannah Burgess divided her time between the ship and her husband. Then, "Nineteen days from Chincha Islands, 250 miles from Valparaiso, and in sight of Juan Fernandez Island, at 11 P.M. my dear husband departed this world apparently at peace with his maker and in no pain." The *Challenger* made port at Valparaiso four days later, on December 15, 1856. Hannah Burgess had been in command for over three weeks.

Exactly one month earlier, on November 15, 1856, the clipper *Neptune's Car* had arrived in San Francisco with another captain's wife in command. Mary Patten had commanded for fifty-two days, successfully navigated the difficult passage westward around the Horn, and dealt with serious problems of discipline as well as a dying husband. When she took command she was nineteen years old and four months pregnant.

Mary Patten was sixteen when she married Joshua A. Patten, the captain of *Neptune's Car*. It was obvious from the beginning of her first voyage with him that she would be a useful addition to the ship's company. The captain went so far as to make a notation in his log that "Mrs. Patten is uncommon handy about the ship, even in weather, and would doubtless be of service if a man." As it was, his wife helped dispense medicines, cooked, and took instruction in navigation. By the end of the voyage it was agreed that Mary Patten could easily pass the examination for a masters' certificate. Her second voyage on *Neptune's Car* would call on all these talents and more.

Neptune's Car left for San Francisco on July 1, 1856, racing with two other clippers. Record passages were important both to captains and to shipowners, so much so that some were tempted to win by unfair means. There had been newspaper reports of crew members being planted on a ship by an opposition line to sabotage the race. *Neptune's Car* appeared to have such a saboteur in its chief mate, a man named Keeler. He was insubordinate, abused the crew, and the captain discovered that he pulled in sail when he had the watch, to slow the ship, and slept on duty. Within a few weeks, Keeler was put in irons and the captain took over his watches. He did not dare to promote the second officer into Keeler's slot because the man was illiterate and knew nothing of navigation.

As *Neptune's Car* approached the Horn, Captain Patten kept the deck day and night and then began battling the strong westerly gales. The wet, cold, and exhaustion finally were too much for him. His hearing and eyesight failed, and he was put to bed, raving deliriously. From his place of imprisonment, Keeler, learning that the captain had been disabled, demanded to be released and given command. The alternative, he pointed out, was to give command to a nineteen-year-old girl, who obviously was unfit to assume such responsibility.

Mary Patten disagreed. She had the support of the second mate and believed the crew would trust her more than they would an officer who slept on his watch. She sent a message to Keeler, telling him that her husband did not trust him when he was well, and she would not trust him now that her husband was sick. Keeler attempted to rouse the crew to mutiny, but Mary Patten had correctly assessed the situation. She made a speech to the crew, assuring them that she could get them safely to San Francisco as long as she had their support, and they believed her.

Then they took on the Horn. For fifty nights Mary Patten slept in her clothes. During one forty-eight-hour period she was constantly on the quarterdeck, wearing oilskins for protection against the spray and watching anxiously for the moment, which must be seized immediately, when it would be safe to hoist some sail. Repeated efforts to hoist sail failed; as soon as a sail was set it was torn to ribbons. Mary Patten continued to fight the elements, shouting orders through a speaking trumpet and keeping the ship's head up to the sea. Finally, after two days, the wind eased enough to allow a little canvas to be spread. At last they rounded the Horn.

Mary Patten made a neat record in the log as progress was made at last: "A hard beat to the windward under reefed topsails and foretopmast staysail."

Meanwhile, Captain Patten seemed somewhat improved. Although he could not leave his bed, he decided to release Keeler. That was a mistake. Exactly what happened is not clear, but Keeler appears to have attacked the captain's wife. The men on watch heard cries and were told there had been a "dreadful accident"; Keeler was lying across the entrance to the cabin with a lump on his forehead. It was also discovered that Keeler had changed course; instead of continuing the race to San Francisco, he had given orders directing *Neptune's Car* to the port of Valparaiso. That was the end of Keeler's freedom; he spent the rest of the voyage in the brig and was taken to jail in San Francisco.

But there was still a way to go before *Neptune's Car* would reach her final destination. And there was still a race to win. Mary Patten crowded on sail; one day *Neptune's Car* logged over three hundred miles. Then, heartbreakingly, with San Francisco only a few days away, the winds failed and the ship lost ten days when the sails were useless. *Neptune's Car* had once made the passage from New York to San Francisco in only 97 days; this voyage took 136. Still, it was respectable time, and *Neptune's Car* came in second in the three-ship race.

When *Neptune's Car* anchored in San Francisco harbor, however, it was not her speed but her commanding officer's sex that interested those on shore. Mary Patten's story was soon known all over the world. She received a gift of $1000 from the insurance company that underwrote *Neptune's Car,* together with a laudatory letter, which read in part: "We know of no instance where the love and devotion of a wife have been more impressively portrayed than in your watchfulness and care of your husband during his long, painful illness. Nor do we know of an instance on record where a woman has been called upon to assume command of a large and valuable vessel, and exercised a proper control over a large number of seamen, and by her own skill and energy impressing them with a confidence and reliance making all subordinate, and obedient to that command." Leaders of the women's rights movement were ecstatic, pointing to Mary Patten as living proof that there was nothing women could not do.

Mary Patten did not become involved in the women's rights movement, however. She had her pregnancy and a very sick husband to worry about. The baby was born on March 10, 1857, and the captain died three months later. Suddenly she was a mother, a widow, and unemployed. Well-wishers raised a fund of $1400 for her, but something seemed to have gone out of her. She contracted typhoid fever and then came down with tuberculosis. Mary Patten died at the age of twenty-three. But she was not forgotten. She was certainly the outstanding woman in the history of the U.S. Merchant Marine, and the hospital at the Merchant Marine Academy at Kings Point, New York, still bears her name.

6

A New Day Dawning

FROM THE TIME of the French Revolution an enormous amount of writing on "women's rights" was accompanied by considerable social and legal reform in both Europe and America. So great did the progress of women appear to contemporaries that the early years of the twentieth century were hailed as the beginning of a new era in human history, the age of the "new woman."

Eight decades later, women are still unrecognized as equal under the law. With both men and women conscious of economic discrimination against female workers, the conviction of Americans, in the opening years of the century, that women had at last achieved all their desired rights and freedoms seems sadly quaint. Yet there was reason at the time for self-congratulation.

In the last half of the nineteenth century women had broken down all sorts of barriers. While education had once been denied to girls, for fear it would damage their health to stimulate their brains, girls in 1900 went to

school and studied such subjects as chemistry and biol-
ogy with no visible ill effects. Some girls from wealthy
families took it for granted that they would go on to
college as well, many of them studying in coeducational
institutions. A tiny number of women even went to
professional schools and studied law and medicine.

While women of the working class had previously been
confined to jobs as seamstresses or domestic servants because it was assumed that the modesty of their sex would
make it impossible for them to function in public places,
women had gradually been accepted as schoolteachers,
factory workers, waitresses, and salesclerks. Women had
proved themselves capable — working under male supervision — of operating such dangerous and stress-
producing modern devices as the typewriter, telegraph,
and telephone and had come to be accepted in business
offices. Even before the turn of the century some western states had given women the right to vote, to serve on
juries, and to hold such public offices as sheriff. The
women's suffrage movement, once considered impossi-
bly radical, was gaining momentum and it seemed it
would be only a matter of time before the entire nation
would recognize the political equality of the sexes.

What would the twentieth century have to offer seafaring women? Would they enter the merchant marine
and the navy in new roles? Could they, like men, aspire
to seagoing careers without first marrying a captain or
disguising their sex? The quiet assumption of many
shipboard duties by wives at sea was not widely known,
so to land-based feminists command at sea seemed, in

the nineteenth century, the most extreme conceivable
example of female emancipation. In 1845 Margaret
Fuller, the feminist theorist, wrote, "You ask me what
use will she make of liberty when she has so long been
sustained and restrained? . . . If you ask me what offices they may fill, I reply — any. I do not care what
case you put; let them be sea captains, if you will." Yet
in 1906 Gertrude Lynch wrote an article entitled
"Yachtswomen of America" for *Cosmopolitan*, suggesting that the day of female sea captains had arrived.

Lynch recognized that it was still uncommon for a
woman to command a vessel of any sort. "It is true,"
she wrote, "that there are thousands of . . . women who
recline at ease upon the deck with no other thought than
that their gowns are suitable for the occasion, their co-
quetries assured; who lose sight of the mental enjoyment of controlling elemental forces just as they are blind
to the colors of sky and sea. They may even be in the
majority, but the majority are rarely worthy of description." Lynch directed her attention to a different sort of
woman, one "tense in muscle as in purpose, with a clear
eye fixed on a far horizon or studying the quadrant at
her side. She arranges her own wind-blown draperies
and she knows when to reef a sail and when to take
advantage of the caprices of wind and current."

Women had long been accepted in schools for navigators, and Lynch pointed out that there were classes
especially designed for women "in which they have
learned not only the mystery of knots, bends and splices,
but how to keep a locker as neat as a work-basket, the

manipulation of rigging and sail and the handling of various kinds of pleasure craft, from the natty catboat, raceabout and knockabout to the more formidable cutter, yawl, schooner, brigantine and even the full-rigged ship." There was apparently something addictive about maritime studies, and women, once they began them, continued to extend their areas of competence. "Like the novice housekeeper who begins by dusting furniture and ends by studying the mechanism of furnace and boiler," Lynch wrote, "so the yachtswoman has taken, it would seem, all knowledge of seamanship for her possession."

After learning to handle small craft, women studied for and passed examinations qualifying them for the certificate awarded to a first-class navigator, which attested "that the holder has mastered the mysteries of all practical problems in geo- and celo-navigation and may safely be entrusted to navigate a vessel around the world."

Furthermore, Lynch added with a trace of smugness, women who had been licensed as navigators, pilots, and even masters of steamships proved to be excellent sailors. "Strange as it may read to those who class women as careless, capricious beings, not a single report of accident, where the fair skipper has been at fault, has ever been recorded against a craft that has sailed with a woman at her helm. This truth is attested to by all those who have taught women seamanship and navigation. It is said by these authorities that they are careful of consequences; they obey orders without question and in addition are not apt to tamper with the possibilities of accident that lurk in the cup that cheers to such an extent that its soundings are measured too often for prudence."

Lynch lists a large number of women qualified for command on both working ships and pleasure craft, adding chauvinistically, "There is no country in the world which can boast such a list of practical yachtswomen as America." Other nations, unfortunately, were childishly narrow-minded. With a hint of condescension, Lynch described the experience of Lady Ernestine Brudenell Bruce with the English authorities. She was an experienced yachtswoman, well trained in seamanship and navigation, but when Lady Ernestine applied to take the examination for an English yachting license, "Her application was refused on the ground that the board of trade recognized the word 'master' as applying only to the male sex, and so declined to entertain her name for the eligible list." The contrast with American practices, Lynch added, "need not be further insisted upon than by a simple narration of fact."

Why did women want to qualify as ships' captains? Lynch believed the most important reason was simply the pleasure of command. "The mountain climber can never make those who stand at the foot or midway on the slope believe that the view from the summit has doubly repaid his exertion. It is the mysterious secret of achievement that only the laurel-crowned can understand what they have really gained. The mental quickening which comes to the master of craft is as distinct an enjoyment as the feel of the fingers on the wheel, the salt spray against the cheek, the thrill that comes when the vessel, like a bird obeying the call of the fowler, leaps to the hand and crosses the line one minute ahead of the near-by rival." The photographs of women at the helms of their racing yachts — "the masculine element conspicuous by its absence or subordinate presence" — which accompany the article confirm Lynch's assertion that a good reason to want the license is that controlling such craft is fun.

That, however, was not the only reason women sought the license. In addition to "women of the leisure class whose effort has for *ultima thule* their own enjoyment or the rivalry of sex against sex" who proudly displayed a master's certificate elaborately framed in the cabin of a pleasure yacht, "many a woman of different standing in the social and financial world displays it no less zealously, in strongbox or neatly arranged locker; to her it is the synonym of a bank account, the security of tried abilities, a part of the practical equipment of her profession."

Lynch discovered that a substantial number of women were making a living as captains of riverboats and vessels carrying both passengers and freight on the Great Lakes, the Chesapeake Bay, and Long Island Sound. "According to marine statistics," she reported, "there are a large number of our river, sound and lake boats, both passenger and freight, captained by the so-called gentler sex — the word is almost a misnomer when applied in this context." Perhaps anticipating a bit of skepticism, she added, "The history of the water attests

that they are well commanded, a fact which may be believed as recorded, for if chivalry does not stand shiv-
ering on the brink its fingers are certainly too numb to
alter the register of marine events."

These working women, Lynch observed, appeared
totally oblivious to the fact that an outsider might be
surprised to find them in a normally masculine role.
They were just doing a job and were in no way engaged
in a "rivalry of sex against sex." "The most careless
observer," Lynch wrote, "could not avoid being as much
attracted by the lithe and supple motions of hand and
wrist on the wheel, the keen outlook on the chessboard
of tangled shipping as by the absolute unconsciousness
of the fact that they are doing anything extraordinary.
They are . . . doing unusual things in a usual way and
when off duty exchanging recipes for ginger cake."

After mentioning Mrs. S. E. Ballard, captain of the
Mississippi steamboat *Lola*, Mrs. Mary Greene, captain
of the *Greenland* (who would remain a riverboat captain
for more than fifty years, from 1896 to 1949), and Miss
Carrie B. Hunter, who was licensed master of the
steamer *Carrie* on the Chesapeake Bay, Lynch described
the commander of *Marengo*, a six-hundred-ton schooner
carrying cargo on the Great Lakes. She was "Miss Lillian McGowan, who, at the ripe age of sixteen, with her
hair falling in a braid down her back, careless of the
fripperies of her sex and youth, can not only give orders
to the crew about her as to the proper passage and land-
ing of the vessel, but when her orders are not executed

promptly enough, can turn to and execute them herself."

In her enthusiasm, Gertrude Lynch went so far as to argue that any woman who contemplated traveling at sea for any reason would do well to study seamanship and navigation and equip herself with a master's license. "The question is often asked," she wrote, "as to what possible advantage it can be to a woman to hold a certificate as master, captain or pilot on a vessel thoroughly equipped with well-paid and competent officers. The answer to this question is . . . that in no situation in life is there such probability of accident, no such chance to avert discomfort, at least, by knowledge and skill and presence of mind as on board ship. A thorough grounding in seamanship and navigation is a trusty staff; it may never be needed it is true, but its possession spells security." To support this assertion, Lynch cited the experience of one Miss Thoms, a passenger aboard a merchant vessel whose regular officers were incapacitated. She navigated the ship around Cape Horn and brought it into San Francisco Bay. Her example, Lynch observed, "has been seconded by other women in other circumstances."

Readers of Lynch's article, published three quarters of a century ago, might well have concluded that the place of women as mariners was so firmly established that within a few years they would be as much a part of seafaring activities as men. Of course, it did not work out quite that way. Opportunities for women actually

narrowed for a time; and in the closing decades of the
twentieth century, women at sea are still far from equality with men, either in numbers or in status. Nevertheless, during the past decade opportunities for women
have expanded again; a capable and determined woman
can now reasonably aspire to fill virtually every role at
sea in any kind of craft if she works for her goal hard
enough and wants it badly enough to persist in the teeth
of sexist prejudices that are a long way from becoming
extinct. The history of seafaring women is just beginning; the golden age of seafaring, in which gender is
irrelevant, is still in the future.

Captains' wives were a group of seafaring women that
went into noticeable decline in the twentieth century.
As steamers replaced sailing vessels, shorter voyages may
have made separation more tolerable. It continues to be
perceived as a hardship, however, by both husbands and
wives. A. G. Course, the historian of the British merchant navy, wrote in 1963, "The monetary reward to a
seafarer has undoubtedly improved, as has his living
conditions on board; but can anything compensate for
the loss of home life, and for the companionship of those
loved ones who must stay ashore? The sea was his first
love; but it is not always his last." Probably the virtual
disappearance of officers' families from British and
American merchant vessels occurred as corporations replaced individual master-owners, so that the personal
desires of the captain and his wife no longer carried de-
cisive weight. After World War II, British oil-tanker
companies led the way in permitting wives of their cap-

tains and chief engineers to go to sea with them, and today families of many nations again make their homes on deepwater commercial ships.

Women remained aboard longer on smaller merchant craft, especially harbor boats and inland steamers. Daisy May Godfrey became a captain's wife in 1911 and set up housekeeping on a New York tugboat. After she earned her navigator's license, Captain Godfrey signed her on as second mate. She continued to study and eventually earned a master's license. During World War II the Godfreys were aboard an ocean-going tug that was part of the Moran fleet. Once they were caught in Boston Harbor for several hours during a U-boat scare while the submarine nets were down. Daisy May Godfrey was awarded the North Atlantic Star and the Merchant Marine Bar.

On the cargo barges of the Mississippi, Ohio, Illinois, Missouri, Arkansas, and Tennessee rivers, women cooks remained fairly common. In the popular history and legend of riverboats they were as invisible as women ever were at sea. The few who made reputations as colorful characters gave the majority a stereotypic image they neither deserved nor desired. Far from being hard-drinking viragos who rustled cattle and shot their lovers during their time on shore, they tended to be grand-motherly types who made the job of riverboat cook a thoroughly conventional feminine role. Hundreds of women hold such jobs today. They are usually the only females aboard, and they put in twelve- to fourteen-hour days that begin long before dawn. Although they are working crew, not captains' wives, the riverboat cooks naturally assume the role of mother to the men. "They'll bring their little family troubles to you," said fifty-nine-year-old Virginia Springer, who began working on the river when she was in her thirties. "You have to mother them. They'll even ask you about the clothes they wear on deck. They're all kids to me." Violet Roberts, who had twenty-four years of experience on the river when she retired at the age of sixty in 1980, said retirement was going to be hard. "I don't know whether I can turn my boys over to someone else," she said. And "the boys" generally appreciate having such a mother figure around: "A lady on the boat really makes a difference," one deckhand was quoted as saying in 1978. "I've worked on some boats with male cooks and there is more tension. The guys aren't as nice to one another."

Women first joined the crews of ocean-going vessels in similar feminine roles. By the end of the nineteenth century it was no longer necessary for a woman to disguise her sex to get a seagoing job. Indeed, aboard passenger ships certain jobs became exclusively feminine — stewardess, nurse, masseuse, librarian, beautician, waitress, and baby sitter have been pink-collar occupations afloat, as they are on shore, for a century.

During World War II, all American women sailors were beached, much to their chagrin, because, as they pointed out, British, Russian, and Norwegian women were helping the war effort at sea. The Russians even had women in their "naval infantry," the amphibious combat force. The National Maritime Union, although it had only four hundred women members, supported their request to return to sea — not as stewardesses and waitresses, but as radio operators, cooks, storekeepers, and pursers' clerks. Although these women sailors were making more money in new jobs as welders or aircraft mechanics than they would at sea, they were more than willing to take a pay cut to get closer to the action. When twenty-two-year-old Irene Walker was asked why she was willing to give up a job paying four times what she had earned at sea, she answered simply that she and her friends "thrive on danger." But neither coast guard nor navy women were permitted to go to sea during World War II, and the women of the merchant marine were kept on the beach as well. Navy nurses could go to sea, however, and a number of those women were killed (some in kamikaze attacks), wounded, or made prisoners of war by the Japanese.

In England, where the war pressed closer to home, women of the merchant marine were not banned from serving at sea. Victoria A. Drummond, a qualified engineer, served as second engineer on the S.S. *Bonita* during World War II and was decorated with the M.B.E., Lloyd's Silver Medal, the Coronation Medal, the war medal, and five campaign stars. The official citation for the award from Lloyd's reads: "The ship was attacked for thirty-five minutes by a bomber when four hundred miles from land but by skilful handling many hits were avoided. When the alarm was sounded Miss Drummond at once went below [to the engine room] and took charge. The first salvo flung her against the levers and nearly stunned her. When everything had been done to increase the ship's speed she ordered the engine room and stokehold staff out. After one attack the main injection pipe, just above her head, started a joint and scalding steam rushed out. She nursed this vital pipe through the explosion of each salvo, easing down when the noise of the aircraft told her that bombs were about to fall, and afterwards increasing steam. Her conduct was an inspiration to the ship's company, and her devotion to duty prevented more serious damage to the vessel." After the war Virginia Drummond continued her career at sea, serving as chief engineer on the ships of several countries.

After World War II, female officers and even female captains — especially aboard ships flying Eastern European flags — became numerous enough to irritate male sailors who accepted women on the crew in traditional roles, but were disturbed or threatened by women who behaved as though their gender was irrelevant. Indeed, as American cruise ships, and the American Merchant Marine as a whole, went into a period of decline in the second half of the century, women began to find it difficult to fight their way back to sea, even in conventional feminine jobs.

After the American cruise ships disappeared, Hazel Zuckerman, who had been working as a waitress on a liner since she was widowed at the age of fifty-three, found herself unemployed. As a member of the maritime union, she continued to pay her dues because, she said, "I was no kid and I knew that, as a union member, so long as I passed the physical and was able to work, they were supposed to keep me employed. And they did — that is, while the cruise ships were running." But when the cruise ships were gone, the only jobs for stewards were in tankers, freighters, and container ships, and there were restrictions against hiring women for such jobs. Hazel Zuckerman led a delegation of unemployed women sailors to Washington, where Representatives Margaret Heckler, Patsy Mink, and Bella Abzug arranged for them to have an interview with Admiral Bender of the coast guard. Zuckerman recalled what happened:

"When I asked him about the restrictions against women, he said that women were banned from non-cruise ships because there were no separate toilet facilities for them. Now mind you, this was just sexual prejudice. Women had long been working on foreign ships. I've met Swedish women working cargo vessels and whatever kind of vessels were around. The Norwegian women were working; the Russian women were working; they were all working — but not the American women. 'I've been flying on airplanes,' I told the admiral, 'and I've never seen separate toilets for men and women. There were boys and girls in my family and we turned out all right, with only one bathroom. Did *your* mother have a special bathroom for her boys and for her girls?' He laughed. He had to admit that she didn't . . . And he agreed that the restrictions against women sailing tankers and freighters should be lifted. But now came that old bugaboo — sex. This was one of the things they were very concerned about. 'Listen, admiral,' I told him, 'do I look like a sex symbol to you?' (I had added a few more years to those original fifties.) 'Do you think for one moment that the men are going to chase me all over the vessel trying to rape me, or else that I'm going to start chasing the men all over the vessel trying to rape *them?* Do you think that's likely to happen?' He had to laugh, and finally he said to me 'Well, you've convinced me, Hazel. You've certainly convinced me.' "

When the union sent Hazel Zuckerman out to her first job on a freighter, both the crew and the captain were taken aback, but they had to take her and soon got used to having a mother figure on board. And Hazel Zuckerman meant to be just that; she was no crusading feminist, just a widow who needed to earn a living. "The men were rough diamonds, but they were grand. They cleaned up their language. If a word slipped out here or there, they were very apologetic. Next I said to them, 'What has happened to all that beautiful macramé work that seamen once did? Macramé is the big thing now. I've never seen one of you do anything.' " So she taught them, and eventually there were macramé planters filled with plants all over the ship. Furthermore, she fussed over the food, learning the favorite dishes of each of the men, making sure the eating utensils were thoroughly cleaned, setting the table, and making salads. The crew members were as pampered as if they had been her charges on a cruise ship. When the ship returned to port, Hazel Zuckerman had proved that there was a place for a woman aboard a freighter. The chief engineer wrote to the president of the maritime union: "We get a smile now instead of a dirty look when we ask for second helpings. Send me more Hazels."

Hazel Zuckerman finally got the job she wanted, but she had to fight for it. If there was antagonism toward a woman who wanted to go to sea to fix meals and teach macramé, there has been far more directed toward young women ambitious to fill traditionally male slots. Even here, however, women have made progress in the past decade. In addition to being cooks, a few women have been hired as deckhands on riverboats. In 1977 a woman headed up the engine-room "black gang" of the Great Lakes iron-ore freighter *John S. Dykstra*. Meanwhile, maritime schools, such as those that women who wished to earn navigators' or masters' licenses at the turn of the century had attended, began actively to promote careers for women in the maritime industry and to attract increasing numbers of female students. In 1974 the Merchant Marine Academy at Kings Point became the first of the federal military service academies to accept women.

The graduation of women from the Merchant Marine Academy, with licenses qualifying them as deck or engineering officers and commissions as ensigns in the U.S. Naval Reserve, opened a new chapter in the history of American women at sea: women in uniform qualified for service at sea in wartime in conventionally male roles — not wives, not nurses, not "civilians" who helped out because they happened to be aboard — but regular officers. The opening of the coast guard and navy service

academies to women in 1976 did not immediately extend the opportunities for women ambitious for seagoing careers. Unlike the merchant marine, neither the
coast guard nor the navy permitted women at sea. But
by the mid-seventies it was clear that some radical
changes were on the way.

In 1972 Admiral Elmo Zumwalt startled navy tradi-
tionalists with one of his famous "Z-grams." "I foresee
that in the near future we may well have authority to
utilize officer and enlisted women on board ships," he
wrote. "In view of this possibility we must be in a position to utilize women's talents to help us achieve the
size navy we need under an all volunteer force environment and still maintain the sea shore rotation goals for
all." It took a court order from federal Judge John Sir-
ica in July 1978, however, before navy women could go
to sea. United States Navy women became seafarers for
the first time in November 1978, but they have since
progressed rapidly. They are still, however, banned from
certain specialties and from all assignments aboard defined "combat vessels," except in medical ratings, which
severely limits their career opportunities. Nevertheless,
by January 1980 the navy had its first female surface
warfare officer at sea and growing numbers of enlisted
women. Commanding officers with the fleet appear to
be pleased with their performance and have been asking for more. The captain of the repair ship U.S.S.
Vulcan recalled taking the vessel through a North Atlantic storm "with a female helmsman, a female quarter-
master-navigator, a female phone talker — even a fe-

male officer of the deck — and I was as comfortable and at ease with them as I have ever been in a storm with any ship." Twentieth-century women have also proved themselves as capable of hard physical labor as their sisters of earlier days who went aloft to set sail or carried ammunition in the great wooden warships. A newspaper reporter was surprised to see women sailors on a winter Atlantic cruise who "manhandled heavy, ice-covered deck lines, guided the wheel from the ship's pilot house . . . helped repair ship's machinery in the deep, unfamiliar world that exists below decks, and wrestled 50-pound containers up and down perilously narrow mess-deck ladders."

It is no longer inconceivable that all barriers to women's participation in naval warfare could be dropped in a few years. At present, however, a woman interested in a military career at sea will find greater opportunities with the coast guard. Indeed, of all the military services, opportunities for women are greatest in the coast guard and poorest in the navy. The coast guard first assigned women to sea duty in 1977, dropped all restrictions based solely on gender in 1978, and in April 1980 put a woman in command of the U.S. Coast Guard cutter *Cape Newagen,* making twenty-six-year-old Lieutenant Junior Grade Beverly Kelly the first woman ever to be legal commander of an American warship. It was not a token appointment. Three months later the cutter *Cape Current,* under the command of Lieutenant Susan I. Moritz, carrying out a coast guard mission in waters southeast of Miami, intercepted a cabin cruiser smuggling three thousand pounds of marijuana, valued at $1.1 million. In peacetime the coast guard sees much more action than the navy, which, to some women, may be an additional attraction.

Any woman looking for a career at sea today, in the merchant marine or one of the uniformed services, will face greater difficulties than a man. In addition to legal barriers, which still exist, problems arise because men have difficulty in adjusting to changing roles. As a midshipman at the Merchant Marine Academy put it, the problem is "not so much a woman's inability to perform; women can and do perform well. Rather the problem was with men's inability to perform around women." Fortunately, few men are unable to overcome this disability. Indeed, it is more likely to be shore-based newspaper reporters who bring up the question of gender, and, as a navy public information officer put it, "Only when sailors reach anonymity without reference to their sex can the integration of women into the armed services be called truly successful." "I don't think about the fact that I am a woman too much on board," said a female lieutenant to a journalist who interviewed her because she was the only one of her sex aboard the hydrographic survey vessel *Peirce* in 1977. "Like most other areas in society, the majority of cadets are not unduly concerned about changing male-female roles, even if they aren't exactly sure what the outcome will be," said a female midshipman interviewed at the Merchant Marine Academy in 1981. And when Lieutenant Moritz was asked whether her sex had made any difference to her all-male crew, she replied, "A commanding officer is a commanding officer."

Probably experience and an increasing number of female officers and senior enlisted women at sea will eventually make mixing the sexes on a ship as acceptable as mixing the sexes in a business office, a circumstance once considered equally extraordinary and shocking. At present, however, women who are serious about wanting a career at sea should be forewarned that in most areas they will be pioneers, roles that are never easy.

But one need not go to sea to work. Seafaring is no longer the major occupation in America that it once was, and most people go to sea today for fun. The first cruise ships sailed in the 1890s and were only for the very rich. Today there are still fabulously expensive around-the-world voyages for those who have the time and money, but there are also week-long jaunts on small vessels off the New England coast and one-day excursions in the Chesapeake Bay or from Miami to the Bahamas. Some ships are so large and designed with so little regard to nautical decor that a vacation aboard them scarcely differs from one in a resort hotel; aboard other craft passengers are invited to participate in deck work, hauling lines, chipping paint, and getting splashed by the spray as part of the vacation fun. Some of these vessels are owned and even crewed by women.

Just before World War II, boating became a popular sport for many Americans. Although only a few people own great yachts, many ordinary people charter or are part owners of small sailing craft. They find their greatest pleasure in the battle with wind and waves that was once the serious occupation of generations of fishermen and coasting captains.

For those who like to mix education with their recreation, there are many attractive opportunities. Several institutions of higher learning, including Southampton College of Long Island University and the University of Pittsburgh, offer programs in which students may earn college credits during an ocean cruise. The ships themselves are the curricula on such vessels as the ketch *Argus*, used to train Boy Scouts and Girl Scouts in the craft and mysteries of a sailing ship. The volunteers aboard the *Providence*, a 1976 reconstruction of John Paul Jones's first war command, include women who participate in the re-creation of life aboard an eighteenth-century warship at sea without being required to assume the subordinate status assigned to their sex two hundred years ago. Even handicapped people may participate in seafaring activities. A ship to be known as the *Jubilee* will be launched in England in 1982 to accommodate thirty trainees, eight of whom may be in wheelchairs. And there is a bimonthly journal, *Boating World Unlimited*, for those who love the sea and refuse to be parted from it because of a physical handicap.

Some modern seafarers go to sea with a mission. Volunteer maritime researchers take working vacations coordinated by Earthwatch, a nonprofit organization based in Belmont, Massachusetts. "Our goals are straightforward," writes President Brian Rosborough. "We encourage the pursuit of knowledge and involve more people in the search for answers which may improve the quality of life." You need not be an expert to join; volunteers are taught what they need to know and young people between sixteen and twenty-three can compete for scholarships to join an expedition. Others must pay their way to the site. Earthwatch volunteers may vacation on small boats, measuring ocean currents off Bermuda, studying the flora and fauna of the Great Barrier Reef of Australia, recording the behavior of humpback whales in the Caribbean, or studying the same mammals in another expedition based in Hawaii.

Greenpeace goes beyond studying whales and takes action to halt the hunting of this endangered species. In 1981 Greenpeace had two vessels, *Rainbow Warrior* and *Rainbow Warrior II*. Women have made up as much as one-third of the crew on Greenpeace ships. Women have also served aboard *Sea Shepherd* and *Sea Shepherd II*, not affiliated with Greenpeace, which pursue the same mission. The crews of these ships take aggressive, but nonviolent, action against the ships hunting whales, often putting their own vessels and their own bodies between the whale hunters and their prey. "The Greenpeace ethic," runs the organization's statement of purpose, "is not only to personally bear witness to atrocities against life; it is to take direct action to prevent them. While action must be direct, it must also be nonviolent. We must obstruct a wrong without offering personal violence to its perpetrators. Our greatest strength must be life itself, and the commitment to direct our own lives to protect others." Crew members on save-the-whale ships must pay their own way, and some might consider that a peculiar form of vacation. Denise Dowdall, who worked in the engine room of *Sea Shepherd II*, said, "It seems we're always covered with grease, and down below, where it smells of cod liver oil." There is sometimes the disappointment of cruising for a season without ever encountering a whaling vessel. That happened to Michi Mathias who, at eighteen, was one of the seven women aboard the Greenpeace vessel *Ohana Kai* in 1977. Still, there are satisfactions to be gained by sailing the seas with a mission that can never be experienced by those on a pleasure cruise aboard a luxury liner. "Sometimes it feels like i've been living here forever," Mathias wrote in her journal. "i never think about another kind of existence. I am so happy to be here instead of doing anything else . . . i could be sitting in a square classroom, but here i am floating in the Pacific Ocean somewhere . . . It's beautiful to be here, to be actually living life for awhile."

Sailing the seas for adventure continues to attract women as well as men to the oceans of the world in the twentieth century. In the past decade alone all sorts of things have been done at sea for the first time. Not only have many sail racing records been set, but young couples have crossed the Atlantic and Pacific oceans in rowboats! The first woman to cross the Atlantic solo did it in 1972; in 1977, twenty-eight-year-old Naomi James took a fifty-three-foot yacht around the world nonstop, single-handed, and in record time.

Those who wish to may still find adventure and danger at sea, but the technological advances of the twentieth century have made it possible to find serenity and peace as well. Mystical experiences at sea are still common, especially for those who sail alone or as couples in small craft. The moon, the stars, and sunsets all seem more vibrantly real when viewed over the waves many miles from land. Although most people would find it lonely, others have found that going to sea alone is, for them, an ideal life. Fifty-eight-year-old Ann Gash, who believes she has spent more time sailing the oceans of the world alone than any other woman, is one of these. From June 1975 to December 1977 she sailed alone around the world. In 1981 she was interviewed in Los Angeles on her way back to Australia after she had taken her twenty-six-foot wooden-hulled sailboat *Stella Ilimo* from Australia to California by way of Tahiti, Hawaii, and San Francisco. Mother of six and grandmother of seven, Ann Gash took up sailing in 1974 and feels completely at home alone at sea. The *Stella Ilimo* carries a three-month supply of food, including thirty-five gallons of water and six bottles of rum. Gash also sails with a flute and sixty books. She lives a simple, happy life. "I'm never lonely," she told a reporter. "I read an average of a book a day, write letters, and spend time playing my flute." Sailing alone over the oceans of the world, said Gash, is her way of staying young.

Suggestions for Further Reading

Index

Suggestions for Further Reading

GENERAL

Albion, Robert G. *Naval and Maritime History — A Bibliography,* 4th ed. Mystic, Conn., 1972.

Laing, Alexander. *Seafaring America.* New York, 1974.

Morton, Harry A. *The Wind Commands.* Middletown, Conn., 1975.

Nautical Museum Directory, 5th ed. New York, 1982.

Snow, Edgar Rowe. *Women of the Sea.* New York, 1962.

CHAPTER 1

Baker, Margaret. *The Folklore of the Sea.* London, 1979.

Beck, Horace. *Folklore and the Sea.* Middletown, Conn., 1973.

Benwell, Gwen, and Waugh, Arthur. *Sea Enchantress.* New York, 1965.

Colcord, Joanna Carver. *Sea Language Comes Ashore.* Cambridge, Md., 1945.

CHAPTER 2

Botting, Douglas. *The Pirates*. Alexandria, Va., 1978.
Carlova, John. *Mistress of the Seas*. New York, 1964.
Gollomb, Joseph. *Pirates Old and New*. New York, 1928.
O'Brien, William. *A Queen of Men*. London and Dublin, 1958.
Schonhorn, Manuel, ed. Daniel Defoe. *A General History of the Pyrates*. Columbia, S.C., 1972.
Snow, Edgar Rowe. *True Tales of Pirates and Their Gold*. New York, 1953.

CHAPTER 3

Bassett, Marnie. *Realms and Islands: Journal of Rose de Freycinet*. London, 1962.
Lewis, Michael. *A Social History of the Navy*. London, 1960.
Medlicott, Alexander, Jr., ed. *The Female Marine*. New York, 1966.
Pope, Dudley. *Life in Nelson's Navy*. Annapolis, Md., 1981.
Stivers, Reuben Elmore. *Privateers and Volunteers*. Annapolis, Md., 1975.
Van Denburgh, Elizabeth Douglas. *My Voyage in the United States Frigate "Congress."* New York, 1913.
Warner, Oliver, ed. *Jack Nastyface: Memoirs of an English Seaman*. Annapolis, Md., 1973.
Whipple, A. B. C. *Fighting Sail*. Alexandria, Va., 1978.

CHAPTER 4

Garner, Stanton, ed. *The Captain's Best Mate*. Providence, R.I., 1966.
Riggs, Dionis Coffin. *Far Off Island*. New York, 1940.

Whipple, A. B. C. *The Whalers*. Alexandria, Va., 1979.

Whiting, Emma Mayhew, and Hough, Henry Beetle. *Whaling Wives*. Boston, 1953.

Williams, Harold. *One Whaling Family*. Boston, 1964.

CHAPTER 5

Allen, Oliver E. *The Windjammers*. Alexandria, Va., 1978.

Belano, James W. *The Log of the Skipper's Wife*. Camden, Me., 1979.

Duncan, Fred B. *Deepwater Family*. New York, 1969.

FreeHand, Julianna. *A Seafaring Legacy*. New York, 1981.

Greenhill, Basil, and Giffard, Ann, eds. *Women Under Sail*. New York, 1971.

Linklater, Elizabeth. *A Child under Sail*. Glasgow, 1977.

Mjelde, Michael J. *Glory of the Seas*. Middletown, Conn., 1970.

Snow, Alice Rowe. *Log of a Sea Captain's Daughter*. Boston, 1944.

CHAPTER 6

Atkinson, Jenni. *A Girl Before the Mast*. London, 1977.

Benton, D. X. *Sea Careers*. New York, 1970.

Calvery, J. *The Naval Profession*. New York, 1971.

Compton, Grant. *What Does a Coast Guardsman Do?* New York, 1968.

Fahnestock, Mary Sheridan. *I Ran Away to Sea at Fifty*. New York, 1939.

Fairfax, John, and Cook, Sylvia. *Oars Across the Pacific*. New York, 1973.

Gash, Ann. *A Star to Steer Her By*. Sydney and Melbourne, 1980.

James, Naomi. *At One with the Sea*. London, 1979.
Lewis, David. *Daughters of the Wind*. London, 1967.
Stevenson, Janet. *Woman Aboard*. Novato, Cal., 1981.
Walker, Nicholette Milmes. *When I Put Out to Sea*. New York, 1972.

Index

Lawrence, Minnie, 132-33, 135-36, 137, 140, 145-46, 154
Lawrence, Samuel, 140
Lewis, Ethelinda, 108
Lewis, Valentine, 108
Library of Congress, 99
Little Seal, 81
Lloyd's of London, Silver Medal of, 196, 215-16
Lola, 210
Long Island University, Southampton College of, 224
Lovell, Mary, 46
Lovell, William, 57-58, 59
Low, James, 93
Low, Melancthon Woolsey, 93, 95-96
Lucretia Wilkerson, 158
Lydia, 155
Lynch, Gertrude, "Yachts-women of America," 206-11

McGowan, Lillian, 210
Ma Chua, 7-8
McKenzie, Daniel Tremendous, 74, 75
McKenzie, Mrs. Daniel, 74
Magical charms and rituals, 9-11, 12, 14

Magruder, Thomas C., 94-95
Mama Cocha, 6
Manhattan, 174
Marengo, 210
Mariner's Mirror, 75
Maritime schools, female students at, 219
Marquis of Ely, 51
Maryland Council of Safety, 91
Mathias, Michi, 226
Mauretania, 5
Mayhew, Caroline, 128, 160
Mayhew, William, 160
Mellen, Kate, 153
Melville, Herman, 159-60; *Moby Dick*, 107; *White Jacket*, 107
Men, women disguised as: on warships, 83-87, 88-91, 96-99, 155; on whalers, 154-58; in merchant marine, 184-88
Menstruating women, myths about, 16
Merchant marine: ships, crews of, 169-72; women discouraged from enlisting in, 184; women disguised as men in, 184-88

Merchant Marine, U.S., 169, 203, 216

Merchant Marine Academy (Kings Point, New York), 203, 219, 222

Merchant Marine Bar, 213

Merchant marine captains, wives of (at sea), 162-64; living quarters of, 164-66; advantages enjoyed by, 166-67, 188; journals of, 166-67; servants of, 167; meals served to, 167-68, 169; social status of, 169; children of, 171-73, 174-76, 179-84; childbirth by, 173-74; pastimes of, 177-78; work done by, 188-95; navigation by, 195-96; clipper ships commanded by, 196-203; decline of, 212

Miller, Betsy, 183

Miller, W., 183

Minerva, 9

Mink, Patsy, 217

Miss Liberty tattoo, 12

Mitchell, 156-57

Moonraker, 46

Moore, Elizabeth, 77-78

Moritz, Susan I., 221, 222

Morris, Richard Valentine, 92-93

Mutiny, 194-95

Myres, Mrs., 93

National Maritime Union, 214

Nautilus, 113-14, 133, 138, 141, 144

Naval Reserve, U.S., 219

Navigation: by women on whalers, 158-60; by wives of merchant marine captains, 195-96

Navy, United States, 12, 220; women on warships in, 91-103 *passim*

Navy Department, 93, 94

Navy Nurse Corps, 101

Nelson, Horatio, 71, 72

Neptune, 7

Neptune's Car, 199-202

Nereids, 7

Nereus, 7

New Orleans, 99

Nichols, Hannah Damewood, 95-96

Nichols, Mrs., 102-3

Nichols, Robert N., 95-96

Nicholson, John B., 94

Nile, Battle of the, 74, 76

North Atlantic Star, 213

Whalers (*continued*)
149-51; emergencies confronted by, 151-53; disguised as men, 154-58; nautical skills cultivated by, 157-60
Whales: right, 105; sperm, 105, 124; killer white, 107; humpback, 124, 225; action to halt hunting of, 225; studying, 225
Whirlwind, 166, 197-98
Whitney, Hannah, 89
Widows' walks, 106
Wilkinson, John (pseud.), 99
William H. Connor, 192
Williams, Eliza: her recollections of life on board whaler *Florida*, 108-16 *passim*, 123-35 *passim*, 139-42, 146-52 *passim*, 159; children born to, at sea, 130-31
Williams, Mary, 159

Williams, Thomas W., 159
Williams, Willie, 132, 137, 141, 142-43, 151-52, 159
Women's rights, progress in, 204
Woolsey, Melancthon Taylor, 93, 95-96
World War II, women sailors in, 214-16
Worth, Jane, 130
Wylie, Elinor, "Sea Lullaby," 3
Wynne, Betsey, 72

Xerxes (Persian king), 55, 56

Yachtswomen, American, 206-11
Young, Betsey, 101

Zuckerman, Hazel, 216-19
Zumwalt, Elmo, 220